I0670552

Mixed Emotions

(UN)LOVED

KATY HUNTER

(Un)Loved
ISBN # 978-1-83943-775-5
©Copyright Katy Hunter 2022
Cover Art by Erin Dameron-Hill ©Copyright March 2022
Interior text design by Claire Siemaszkiewicz
Totally Bound Publishing

(UN)LOVED

Dedication

To everybody out there who doesn't always feel it, know that you are loved.

Acknowledgements

I would like to thank everybody at Totally Bound, especially Jamie Rose, my editor, for helping me share this story with the world and putting up with my dreadful punctuation.

Chapter One

I throw the last of my stuff into my bag, check around to see if I've forgotten anything, and head for the door.

This film is done, and with it, my life here. Not my actual life — I'm not going to die or anything — just the person I've become over the last few months.

The lovesick teenager. The grown woman. The friend. The colleague.

All that gets packed up in a box and reinvented for the next shoot.

Time to get drunk, get my party on and maybe make a few terrible sexual decisions before going home.

I walk out of my work trailer — about to tick off the first thing on that to-do list — when my co-star, all-around hot guy and quencher of thirsts, Gil Carter, completely throws me by being on the other side of the door, stopping me dead in my tracks.

This is not part of the plan. Damn it, G.

"Shee." He glances down at the bags in my hands. "Oh, you're already leaving?"

"Yeah, I wanted to get a head start on packing up."
And moving on.

He rubs the back of his neck, avoiding my regard, like he's pissed at me. "I…uh…I got you something." He reaches into the battered canvas messenger bag that he totes everywhere—the one which makes him look like a hot history professor, or at least how I imagine a hot history professor.

In my mind he's wearing one of those tweed jackets with the elbow patches, tight button-up jeans and suede shoes. He's rushing to a lecture, in the rain, holding that scruffy old bag over his head to protect his unruly curls. I open the door for him, my hair held up in a messy bun by a well-placed pencil, my glasses sliding off my nose. *"Oh, Professor…"*

Sigh.

That man does impeccably good hair. He has a mass of curls softer than a kitten's belly. They tumble into this perfect crown that I, *oh*, I want to run my fingers through and maybe tug at a little when the need arises.

I've had dreams about that hair.

Anyway…I digress. After rummaging around for a couple of minutes, he pulls out the most beautiful brown leather journal.

"This is for your private thoughts, if you need to talk but there's nobody around. And you can write shit about people, and they'll never know." He runs his fingers through that infamous head of hair, still avoiding my gaze.

"What if they read it, though?" I reply, earning me a smile.

"Promise I won't. If you promise to only write nice stuff about me." He glances up at me and ruffles those curls again, sending my lady-parts into meltdown.

I look down at the journal. The only things running through my mind right now are the really, *really* dirty things that I'm going to write about him in this thing.

"Thanks, G." I smile, then, no word of a lie, I punch him in the fucking arm.

Not hard. Just enough to show that we're only friends. Just good buddies. Pals.

"You're welcome." He shrugs and shuffles his feet again. The silence is painfully awkward as we stand there, avoiding each other's gazes. My mind is racing. *Why did I punch him in the arm? Who does that?* It's lucky he didn't get down on one knee and offer me a diamond ring. I might have knocked some teeth out.

Ask him out to dinner. Offer to buy him a drink. Say something... Anything.

Reaching down to open my bag, I unzip it, pop the journal in and look up. "Would you —" But he's already gone.

Why am I like this?

I should have said, *"Maybe I'll write about all the fun things we're going to do together."* Then I could have batted my eyelashes flirtatiously, thrown back my head, giggling in a sexy way. He would have pulled me into his arms...

But no. I went in for the buddy punch.

It's not my fault. No, really, I don't *do* flirting. Dr. K calls it *"intimacy issues"*. She leans back into her brown leather armchair and says things like, *"Did you bond? Are you connecting with people?"* My fist connected with his arm. Does that count?

Don't get me wrong, I'm not a virgin or anything. It's just that I don't like touching people, or, more to the point, I don't like them touching me. Grandma was the only person who ever gave me hugs, and she's gone now. They were earned when I did good at an audition or won a pageant.

There is one kind of flirty thing that we've done. Gil's always loved that I call him G — pronounced 'Jee'. Like it's our little inside joke or something. He also gave me a nickname right off the bat.

It's our thing — or it was. It's over now.

When I call him G, he sort of lights up, like it makes him happy. That's the kind of nice that counts, the kind that gives a girl that fuzzy feeling inside.

There's something very intimate about nicknames. People call me Soph — as if they can't even be bothered to say my whole name — but when someone you're close to creates a new, private name for you, that's another thing entirely.

Especially when the man in question is Gil Carter — the deep-thinker, the philosopher, the person who's kept me sane since the beginning of production.

The object of my *carnal* desires.

Admittedly, if you were one to judge someone by their appearance, and you were unaware of the grubby bag, you might not know what to make of him — Italian leather shoes, tailored trousers and the crispest of shirts. Even on his days off, he looks more like he's just stepped off a Parisian catwalk than a Canadian sound stage.

G's clothes are a whole mood, and that mood is 'best man at a wedding in The Hamptons'.

He always has his nose in a book, and when he doesn't, he's napping, more often than not in my trailer. I've lost count of the number of times he has nodded off on my shoulder while we've been going over our lines, his hair tickling my nose.

I don't mind that kind of intimacy — pure and uncomplicated. He keeps me warm and smells like bergamot—or whatever they put in men's fragrances these days. Manly and a little sweaty. It's a good thing. Trust me.

Like me, he's not a people person. Except the difference is that he's totally okay with it. I'm out here trying to be friendly and 'normal', and he's just doing his thing—and totally pulling it off. There's nothing more attractive than a man who knows what he wants and doesn't care what anybody else thinks. I'd give anything for a spoonful of that confidence.

Our nicknames mean more to me than just words. They're a sign of our friendship, and I count on that far more than I've ever counted on us getting together.

* * * *

August 1, 1 a.m.

So, here it is people, the life and times of Sophie Smith.

Actress, influencer, star.

Also, messy bitch, hairy legs, lives alone—except for her favorite juicer—and is in a personal relationship with Uber Eats.

I haven't written a journal since I was thirteen, and even then, it was just thirsty Ian Somerhalder thoughts.

I would legitimately have run away with a vampire at that point in my life—or a werewolf. Let's not forget my werewolf phase.

Teen-me was freaky, and I miss her. She had guts, confidence and big plans.

Present-me has seven million followers on Instagram—who think my life is perfect—and a bunch of dead plants.

Why did he give me the journal? *Why?* Was it supposed to be like, a thing, or am I reading too much into this? Is it too late to give him a gift?

It's too late, isn't it?

Ugh. I need sleep.

Sleep isn't normally a problem for me. I'm so busy when I'm working. I doze off whenever and wherever I can. Some of my best naps have been on G's couch.

I'd pull the lever to make the bed pop out. G would appear with a bottle of beer in each hand. *"You want to watch a movie?"*

"Sure."

"What time do we have to be on set tomorrow?" He'd yawn and lay his famous crumb-catching blanket down before scooching up the bed to make room for me. The man keeps a clean house. Then he'd hand me a beer. *"Don't spill it."* Once. One single time I'd spilled, like, the tiniest amount. He was never going to let me forget it.

I'd grin and pretend to drop it, making him visibly nervous. Then I'd scroll through my phone. *"Ugh, if you can even call it tomorrow... We're on set in three hours."*

"Stick on The Godfather, *then,"* he'd command, pointing at the DVD player. This man, with his DVDs and his journals and his strange obsession with self-help books... I'd grown up in a small town and didn't always fit in with the city folks, but G had traveled here from the last century. He still fit in better than me, though.

"Again?" We must have watched that movie at least ten times.

He'd ruffle his hair and throw me a smile, knowing that nobody could resist his charm, especially me. *"Oh, go on, please. You can tell me all about that time you went to Comic-Con while we watch."*

G had been nothing if not predictable.

"I've told you that story already," I'd say.

"I know, but I love it. Tell me again." He'd get comfy. This involved one hand slung over his head and the other scratching his abs, his shirt all ruffled up.

I swear, he had no idea of the effect he had on me when he did that — or he did and he simply didn't care.

I'd tell him about mistaking a real actor for someone in cosplay, and how we'd done interview after interview so we never got to see anything anyway, and how people queued in the street overnight just to take a photo with me.

He'd listen and laugh and ask questions, then I'd slump down onto his shoulder, desperately trying to stay awake. My eyes would get heavier, the image would get blurry and I'd fall asleep. He'd wrap his warm arm around me — his chin resting on top of my head — and he would watch the rest of the movie in silence. I still have no idea how it ends.

The movies changed but the couch — and the company — were the same every time.

I wish I were there. I could really do with a good nap right now.

In fact, I wish I were anywhere but here, alone in this empty, echoing apartment, waiting to go back to an empty, echoing house. Two more days and I'm LA bound, and about to be a million miles away from him.

Shit. I really need some sleep, a warm shoulder, a good movie and a friend.

I'm going to miss him terribly, more than I've ever missed anybody I've worked with. And that, my dear Dr. K, breaks my heart.

Chapter Two

"Frigid bitch," mutters the guy standing next to me at the bar. *Jerk.* He turns to his friends and adds, "Didn't like her anyway. Just wanted to fuck a celebrity." It had started with a simple request for a selfie. I get it a lot. The guy was slurring his words and using the bar to prop himself up, but he still thought he had a chance with me.

I'm not frigid or a bitch, and I'm not saying any man doesn't have his chance with me, under the right circumstances.

It's not that I'm closed off to love. I'm closed off to having my ass fondled in a bar by a rude, grabby, drunk stranger.

I pay for our drinks and head back to the table.

"You okay, love?" She may be twenty years older than me, but Lucy knows what it is to be in my shoes. She's been there, done that. It's my turn now.

I'm *not* okay.

"Yeah, I guess. Same old shit. First, the selfie, then the pick-up line, then a quick unwarranted fondle of a part of my body, then complete disgust when it turns out I don't want to sleep with him." There'll be a bitter post on Instagram within minutes, *again*, which I'll have to report, *again*. They never do anything. Report, block, repeat. And so it goes on.

It's the first time I've gone on a girls' night in forever. We've been to this bar with the crew loads of times since we'd started filming, no problem. I thought I'd get away without backup. That'd teach me. The minute we take the men out of the equation, we're easy pickings.

"Forget him. Let's just enjoy ourselves," says Em. That's easy for her to say. She was already tanked when we'd picked her up, as were the other girls. They'd finished shooting days ago and had been partying ever since. Em's a beautiful up-and-coming actress who'd scored a pretty important role for someone just starting out. She's the type of person who online magazines do articles about, telling people to watch out for her because she'll soon be everywhere. They're not wrong. The girl has talent. She also has an ego as big as her eyelashes — and she welds those things on with steel.

I'm not bitter. She can have the fame and everything that goes with it. Such a shame, really, that she thinks of me as competition. It would have been nice to have made a female friend my age on set, someone to share all my adventures with. That doesn't happen a lot in my line of work. People like her see me as a threat.

My last scene was yesterday. That feeling of finally being finished with something that has sucked out all my energy is bittersweet, and yet leaving this new family behind is enveloping me and the darkness is winning.

The hard graft is over…until promo. It's easy to forget your real life when you've worked solidly for months without a break. No more early mornings and late nights, but no more people, no more 'friends'. *You win some, you lose some.* I'm sinking back into my murkier thoughts, just like I do every time I go home.

This is supposed to be a fun night out, remember, Sophie?

I pull out my phone to commemorate the moment and raise my glass. "Cheers." Everyone follows suit, clinking them together in the middle of the table, and we toast the final day.

I message the video to my PR person and, within seconds, it's on all my social media accounts. *Heart emoji, crying face emoji, 'Gonna miss these guys'.*

Got to give the people the content. The fantastic lifestyle. Always going out, having fun, enjoying myself. That's what the fans want to see. I'm living the dream, and people need to know that. *"Nobody likes a Moaning Minnie,"* as my grandma used to say. Then she'd pull up the corners of my mouth and tell me I had to smile. They haven't sunk down since, at least not in public.

I glance over at the creepy guy out of the corner of my eye. He's leering at me, balanced precariously on a barstool. Hopefully, he'll drink himself into a stupor and forget I'm even here. Won't take much. He's as drunk as the girls sitting in front of me.

Chatter rings loud around the table. They're laying bets as to who's going to end up in whose bed tonight at the unofficial wrap party at the lads' house. Em is planning to make her move on someone, and I'm pretty sure I know who it is.

G. The man I so desperately want to end up in bed with me.

It's not like we haven't got any practice in. We've spent fifty-percent of the last couple of months writhing around, naked, in a bed together — in front of a crew of thirty, while wearing vanity pouches, body makeup and occasionally being replaced by a body double. It isn't *that* kind of movie, although it wasn't exactly chaste, either.

The worst of it was that I'd fallen in love with him on the very first day. I'd done all that knowing full well that it would never be real, that I'd never sleep with him in a real bed, alone, just the two of us. *Literal torture.*

He'd come knocking on the door of my trailer on the first day. *"Do you want to kiss? Get it over with?"* It was a common thing between actors. I'd been expecting it, but when push came to shove, I'd been as nervous as hell.

I'd gulped down my fear. *"Sure. I'd love to."* Had he heard the hesitation in my voice? *"Yes. Please. If you want to. I don't mind."* I'd pursed my lips and bitten my tongue to get it to shut the fuck up.

He'd taken me in his arms. It had been awkward and silly, and I'd laughed, which had made it even worse — and he'd cupped my chin as I giggled at him, my eyes open, totally unprepared for the emotion that was to follow. There had been tongue — I wasn't expecting tongue — and biting and nibbling. It had been a real kiss, and it had thrown me for a second, making me balk. Not because I didn't like it... Quite the contrary, it had made me want more.

"Shit, I'm sorry," he'd said as I'd pulled away.

"No, it's fine. I just thought people didn't actually kiss." The pleasure I'd felt, the intensity, it had thrown me completely. That wasn't *supposed* to feel like that, and I wasn't *supposed* to enjoy it. *Totally unprofessional.*

The look on his face—a subtle mix of surprise and amusement—would be stored in the 'humiliation' part of my brain forever. You know, the part that keeps you awake at three a.m., ten years after the fact, going over and over the event.

He must have wondered if this *so-called* actress was for real. *"You've never kissed someone on screen?"*

My mind had whirred. Had it been bad? Had I not known how to kiss?

Oh, God. I'm never going to sleep again, mulling that one over.

"Yeah, I have. I just... They were teen kisses, not adult kisses. PG-13." Kisses that hadn't made me feel like that.

"Well, you're adulting now." He'd chuckled at my naiveté, still cupping my chin as if he were going to go in for another. *"Are you going to be okay with this? The kissing is just the start."*

Was I going to be okay with full-frontal nudity and fake fucking this guy? Who knew? This was the job that would change everything. It was the one that would bring me into playing the roles I'd wanted for a while now.

I had to stop playing sixteen-year-old virgins at some point. For that, I was definitely ready. Another role with pigtails and dungarees at twenty-one years-old would have killed my soul.

It had turned out later that I was perfectly fine playing naked wrestling with G. Far from being intimidating, it'd opened my eyes and made me want more.

That was when he'd suggested we keep it platonic.

Not, you know, that I'd given him any indication that I wanted to be anything other than friends. He'd brought up the subject all by himself—as if it weren't *me* he needed to convince.

"We can't allow ourselves to get carried away, to think we've fallen in love. It's very complicated when co-stars get involved. It can affect their performance."

I'd tried to keep a straight face. I knew what he'd meant, but for a second it sounded like dating me would give him droopy dick.

He'd taken it all so seriously. *Nothing* should affect his performance. G was passionate about acting. He went to classes and symposiums, read all the books. I'd always played it by ear, picked it up on the spot. My career had taken off when I was seven, and I'd always kind of winged it. *To each their own.*

"So, you're just assuming I'm going to fall in love with you?" I'd replied, affronted. The cheek of it.

Of course—like every other girl on the planet who's met this man—I fucking have fallen in love with him. But he doesn't need to know that. The only problem is that I've got no idea how he feels about me—and now Em is on the prowl.

Gil Carter is a catch—arm candy for some, husband material for others. Personally, I don't have specific plans for us. I just want to find out what it's like to fuck that sublime body that has been draped over mine so frequently, teasing and exciting me. I've spent two months learning what makes him tick, watching old movies—his choice, cooking—him, talking—me, all the time, non-stop—jamming to our favorite music. He'd tried in vain to get me to listen to a little classical, but I was boybands all the way. I know I love the person, but I desperately need to see if his cock measures up, too.

What if it's the size of his vanity pouch? Just... What if...?

"Fucking bitch." The slurred insult, loud enough for everyone in the bar to hear, brings me out of my X-rated thoughts. I turn to stare. Drunk-guy is up and off his barstool, and ready to fight me. *Great.*

Lucy grabs my hand. "Don't rise to it, honey. That's how they know they're affecting you." What she actually means is *'show the other cheek in case people get their phones out'*. Sure as hell that if I stand up to him, it'll be on TMZ by the morning.

"Thinks she's too good for people like us." The whole table turns to stare. He staggers over, his mates trying to pull him back. His shirt is half out of his trousers, his hair unkempt. "Whore."

The growl that accompanies the word is terrifying, his ire turning his speech to acid. I grab my phone and look for an exit. There's no getting away from the booth without crossing his path.

The barman walks around the bar, stands between us and winks at me. *My savior.* He'll want a selfie too afterward. I'd bet my life on it.

I clench my fists and steady my breathing before speaking. "Look... I really don't want any trouble. I'm sorry I offended you." Flashing him my biggest smile, I make a suggestion, "Let me buy you a drink, you and your friends. Please, it would be my pleasure." I stand up as I say it, peering around him at his friends. They look like a free drink might help them control him.

The barman turns toward them. "Shots all around? On our friend here."

My tactic works. They grab their sad excuse for a friend and pull him back into their fold, and I used those precious seconds to text someone to get me out of here. My hand hovers over my contacts. *Do I dare?*

Can you come get me?

What's up?

22

I glance over, warily.

A drunken fan.

I'll call you when I'm outside.

He takes no time at all, must have raced down to his car. He and the lads are supposed to be having a few drinks at their place before the party. Does it look weird that I called him? No need to overthink it. G is my friend above and beyond any feelings I have for him. That is, after all, the way he sees me.

Lucy accompanies me to the door after I've made my excuses to everybody, taken a selfie with the barman and paid a hefty bar bill. I promise I'll see them all later.

To be honest, all I want to do is have a long soak in a hot bath then slide under my bedcovers and sleep for the next six months, but I will be missed. Sophie Smith is expected to make an appearance. Somebody always wants a piece of me, even my friends.

G is parked out front. He leans over and opens the door for me with a wide smile but a worried expression on his face. "You good?"

"Yeah. I just want to go home." I get in his car and instantly relax. Is it him or the air-conditioned seats? Both, probably. This summer is freakishly hot, and merely stepping from the bar to the car has brought out a sweat.

He, however, is the good type of hot — like, just showered, just shaved, fresh-clean-shirt hot. I haven't even had time to get washed and changed after work. I was grubby and now I'm sweaty too. It's not a good look.

He smiles, tipping his head to stare straight into my eyes. "You sure you're okay, Shee?"

He's never called me by my name. We'd all got high on the first weekend of shooting, and I'd gotten stroppy with him — can't even remember why now — but he'd referred to me as *'Sheeee-who-must-be-obeyed.'* I'd made such a fuss that the name had stuck. At some point, he'd shortened it to 'Shee.'

"Apparently I'm a frigid whore." I contemplate the contradiction of the insult. "How does that even work?"

He grins. "You can't be both. That's just greedy."

"Should I stick with whore? What do you think?" It's hardly the adjective that came to mind when you wanted to refer to my love life...or frigid. Tumbleweed, on a windy day in the desert was more accurate...or just desert.

"Oh yeah, it's pretty much what we think of you anyway."

The irony of me being celibate for so fucking long and yet, in a second, I'd be a whore for this guy isn't lost on me.

Make me your whore, G.

I really need to work on my thirst for this man.

We go back to his place. He claims that it's because he wants some company, but the hand that had been gripping onto mine since I got in the car convinces me otherwise.

Does he like me? My heart rate rises a little. Am I reading too much into this? *Probably.*

He has rented the place for the whole shoot. Lucy has her own apartment, as do I, but most of the others share houses provided by the production company. Not everybody can afford to live alone.

It's comforting not to have to go back to an empty home. My apartment is piled up with boxes of clothes and unopened cooking equipment in anticipation of my departure. Only my juicer remains unpacked.

I love my juicer. It's one of my closest friends.

"I thought you were having drinks with the lads at their place?"

He throws his keys into a bowl and leans against the kitchen counter. "No. I bailed. I needed sleep."

"Oh shit, and I woke you. I'm sorry." I know exactly how he feels. We'd had four- or five-hour nights for months. Sleep sounded awesome right about now.

He grabs my hand again, squeezes it. "No worries. I was just getting out of the shower when you texted me."

I try not to imagine what that must have looked like, but G's naked body flashes into my mind. The image of it—glistening as he stepped out from under the water—is doing stupid things to my insides. Rivulets of water gliding down his sculpted body… Hands on his hips, he'd shake his head, his dark, curly hair sending droplets flying, like a lone wolf stepping out of a river in the moonlight…all of it in the slowest of motion.

Self-consciousness freezes me to the spot. He's watching me, intensely, as the lurid thoughts flash through my mind. A coy smile creeps onto my face. "Thank you, anyway."

"My pleasure. Do you want a drink?" He leans over and pulls open the fridge door, pondering the options. "I have beer."

"No thanks. Do you know what I really want to do? I want to order in food and watch movies on your couch, while I fall in and out of consciousness."

He tidies a lock of my hair off my face and gently grasps the side of my head. "Are you sure you're okay, Shee?"

I let my head drop into his touch, taking in his warmth and comfort. "I'm tired, that's all. Leave me here, and go to the party. You have a whole queue of women waiting to pounce."

"Really?" His face shows little or no signs of being thrilled at the idea of picking and choosing his date for the night. It's more of a wide-lipped cringe.

"Yeah. Em is making her move on you tonight."

He nods, still not conveying any kind of joy. He could do a lot worse. That girl is going places. "Great. You do, too. I know for a fact that there's someone who's had his eye on you for a while now."

Fuck it. Neither of us wants anybody else. I'm sure of it now. He knows it. I know it. Why didn't we just do the thing? I look up at him, sliding my hand onto his chest. "And is that what *you* want, seeing me in the arms of another man?" His whole body relaxes as if he's breathing out for the first time in months.

"No." He kisses me with the same divine passion as that first time. Only this time I'm ready for it. His grasp on my head tightens enough to hold me to him. We step together. I grip his back, pulling up his shirt to embrace his warm body beneath.

His touch, his embrace, brings only warmth and comfort, not a single shred of fear. I have no issue with his intimacy.

"I want you," he confesses when he finally releases me. "I always have." My stomach does a triple backflip. I could listen to him saying that sentence eternally. It's all I've been waiting to hear.

"And you waited until the last day to tell me." I've been pining for him, fantasizing about him. We could have done this *weeks* ago.

He frowns. "I thought you wanted to keep it platonic."

Unbelievable. "That was *your* idea."

"You could have said no."

What?

I stifle a giggle. "You have a funny way of understanding the concept of consent. *'I think we should remain just friends unless you insist on dating me.'*" My stomach growls. "I need food and a movie and wine. Do you have wine? I would kill for a glass of something chilled right now."

"Madame wants wine, Madame shall have wine." He grabs his phone.

Turning around, I bend over to pull the couch out into a bed, something I've done a hundred times since I met G.

A hand grabs my butt and gives it a squeeze. It's such a ridiculous couple-ish thing to do that it makes me snort with laughter.

Things have changed.

We find an old movie. It's another seventies movie, bursting with wide collars, fast cars and dramatic music. It isn't my thing at all, but we never watch them anyway. We've always talked over them. Tonight though, we eat, we kiss, we eat some more, we fool around.

Yeah, things have definitely changed.

I was already somewhat familiar with G's cock. It had rubbed up against me during one of our many love scenes, doing its best to burst out of its vanity pouch. "*It happens sometimes,*" he'd said, ruining the take, the blush rising in his cheeks as he'd grabbed a pillow and slid it between us. "*Sorry.*" Ever the professional. Ever respectful.

This time I have permission to touch.

Our fooling around is getting to the point where over the clothes fumbling is no longer going to do it for us. "Do you want to fuck?" he asks.

Straight to the point. Cool, cool, cool. "No, God no, I haven't showered, and this body is not sex ready." This body is never *'sex ready'*, and they don't have make-up artists, great editing or body doubles in real life. "I need at least twenty-four-hours' notice before you see me naked."

"Don't say that." He frowns, his tone becoming more serious. "You're beautiful."

"Thank you, but it's still no."

"Whatever you want, no pressure."

See? That is the kind of thing that made me want to sleep with him in the first place. It's a double-edged sword with him — the urge to do it right then and there and the knowledge that he'll see my stubbly legs.

The legs win.

"Doesn't mean we can't do other stuff." I open my blouse and undo his belt and trousers. "I don't know how you can be comfortable in these things. Do you ever wear T-shirts and jeans?"

"When I'm at home." He stutters his words as I lean down and place my whole mouth around his cock. "Fuck. Whoa. Okay, we're doing this."

I lift my head, "You want me to stop?" *Crap. Have I misread the situation?*

"No, no. Nope. All good here." I sink back down. "Fuck, Shee."

Something you can't quite tell from looking at me is that I give good head. I mean, it's not like I advertise it online.

#GivesGoodHead. #Ad.

When I was seventeen, I did a movie, a small role, with a very well-known actress. She taught me how to give blow jobs. The lessons were entirely theoretical — well, except for a rather unfortunate banana. She's botoxed all over now, so that part of her life is probably behind her.

My supple young lips were doing wonders to the tip of G's cock, however. A swirl of my tongue, and he is begging for more. I drop my hand down to his balls, tug and tease at them.

It's all in the reaction, the hurried breaths, the pleasured moans. "*If you listen to what his body is saying, you can work out exactly what it takes to make a man come,*" she'd told me.

"Fu-ck me. Fuck." Frequent use of swearwords is also a common sign of a pleasurable experience.

I take my time, enjoying the touch and feel of G's body. His skin is smooth and taut. His workout regime, as well as his skincare one, is precisely calculated to get the best effect on camera. And my fingers, as they grasp his thighs, are relishing all the spoils.

Despite getting a kick out of G's reaction to my hidden talents, I'm still exhausted. The thrill of making out with him has put me on a high — after such a long wait — but my aching, tired body isn't happy with me one bit.

I put all my efforts into making him come, speeding up only a little, rising and sinking onto his shaft, pulling ever so gently on his balls and wrapping my hand around his cock tight enough to make him moan.

He lifts his crotch, and his body stiffens beneath me. The exhilaration of making him come excites me, and I almost regret bringing it to its natural end. Maybe I shouldn't have been so hasty to say no.

"I'm gonna…" I lift my mouth, finish him off with my hand, placing the very tip of his cock on my breast as he comes. "Holy fucking shitfire!"

Told you I was good.
Started the evening with a jerk, finished it with a jerk off.
I'm not just talented. I'm funny too.

Chapter Three

August 2, 2 a.m.

Neither of us are sleepy, so we get stoned and fall down a deep rabbit hole of self-awareness. Or something. Well, I am. G's just getting high.

"I just want to go to bars and not be insulted by drunken guys who want to sleep with me." It happens more than I want to think about. Like a lot. Like every single fucking time.

"That happens to non-famous people, too. People insult me all the time." He starts to tear up, and I caress his cheek. Bless him, he's off his head.

"Not true. Everybody loves you." He smiles at me. Such a beautiful, soulful smile. "I wish I was horribly hideous, then I could live in a cave by the sea and make seashell necklaces."

"No, you don't." He digs his hand down into my bra and flicks the tip of my nipple. "I would miss your tits."

"I know. I don't really. I just want some time, you know, to get to know the real me."

There aren't many facets to Sophie Smith — minor league child actress, a few film roles, nothing to write home about. Then I got my big break at fourteen and never looked back. Hit after hit came my way — movies, a TV series that had the most dedicated fanbase ever and all the followers a girl could dream of on Insta. You can buy figurines of me, too, those ones with the big head. I'm a household name around the world and yet all I've ever known is this — acting, promo, then acting again. This is me...a pretty basic bitch.

"You're fake?" He holds his fingers up to his face. "Is anything real?"

"You are so high right now." He giggles and falls back onto his pillow, still inspecting his hands. "Listen... I haven't stopped working since I was fourteen. I haven't seen my family for years. I want a break. I need a holiday. I want to stop."

"Well then, take a break. Fake. Break. Fake, break. It rhymes."

"You're kidding, right? You want to see my manager's face when I tell her that." *Ugh.* I'm having a goddamned existential crisis, and all the guy can do is make bad poetry.

He sobers up for a second, just enough to lean into me and whisper, "If you want to start living, you need to be the one to make the change. They work for you, Shee. Remember that. If you need a break, then take a break."

Right. *Damn* right.

And that's how it began. From a stupid conversation on a couch at two a.m. between two exhausted, high people came 'The Hiatus'.

* * * *

9 a.m.

A plan has been formed…a devious one. There is no way in hell that Suzy, my manager, will give me time off. Underhanded sneakiness will be required.

"I'm giving it up…acting. I'm giving it up." I sniff and crack my voice a little more.

Suzy emits the deepest sigh into her phone and slips into full crisis-avoidance mode. She's been my manager forever and is the closest thing I have to family, well, except for my actual family, who are the closest thing I have to people who don't give two-shits about me.

"Sophie, you just made ten million from a frickin' movie, you're twenty-one, in the prime of your life and your career, you're one of the few goddamn celebrities to have made the successful leap from child actor to adult lead without going off the rails — and you want to give it all up? Are you crazy?"

"No. I just… I can't do it anymore. I'm burning out." I cough a little. Is that too much? I don't want her to think I'm sick or anything.

"Take a break. You've got a couple of months until you have to do the publicity for this movie. Take some time off."

What? This shit's actually working. She's right. I *am* a good actress.

I go in for the kill. "I mean, I could take three months off, travel, find myself, fall in love." I perk up just a touch. The battle isn't yet won, but this is the best role of my career so far.

"Oh, honey, you can go eat, pray, sleep with all the men in the world, as long as you come back in a couple of months." She's trying to keep it together, but I know she's gripping the edge of her desk by her nails like she always does when she's nervous about something.

I sob and throw in a little squeal. "You're right. You're *so* right. I'll take some time off. Thank you, Suzy."

Another sigh, this time of relief. "No, thank you, Sophie, for being reasonable."

Sometimes you have to go to Sweden to end up in Australia. My cunning plan has worked.

I FaceTime my PA, tell her that I'll pay her extra for the next couple of months if she keeps my social media alive.

"Are you going to rehab?"

"No. Why do you think I'm going to rehab? Do I look like I need to go to rehab?" I run my fingers through my hair, giving it a little shake, as if it would make me less scruffy.

She gulps, loudly, moves her mouth up and down, no words coming out. "Umm…no, of course not, no. I don't know why I thought that. Sorry."

I end the call and grab a mirror, stare at my face intensely. Why would she think that? Why? *Why?*

God, I need some sleep.

* * * *

8 p.m.

I did not expect to find G on my doorstep, coffee in hand, smile on his face, but here he is.

"Come home with me," he says taking a sip of his mocha latte and strolling into my apartment.

"To LA? I already have a house there."

"No, to the South of France, to my parents' farm."

Whoa. That's kind of serious. He's really stepped it up for the second date.

"France?" They have sandy beaches — and bars, and wine. I've been to Paris before, stopped off on promotional tours, but never the south. Cannes, Nice. It's the perfect escape. The ideal opportunity to purge my soul — or whatever people do on hiatus.

"There'll be nobody for miles. You can lie out under the sun or walk for hours and not meet a single person." The incident from the other night has affected him. He seems more protective around me than he ever was before. I've already forgotten about the incident with the jerk in the bar. It's such a frequent occurrence that it just kind of melded in with all the other times some guy has gotten over-friendly or aggressive…or both.

"You know what? I'd love to." This is exactly what I need. Plus, I'm already imagining sex in the hay barns and frolicking in fields of wheat. I'm pretty sure that's what farmers do in the summer.

What am I even going to wear to a farm? I have two days to prepare several weeks' worth of outdoor clothing, put my shit into storage and run away to France with G.

Chapter Four

August 4, 2 a.m.

Shit. We're getting up early to take stuff out to the storage unit. I can't sleep. I forgot to get my nails done. He'll see my nails and know that I'm not worthy of going out with such an attractive man. He'll find out that I actually don't have a clue what I'm doing, that I'm terrible at doing my own makeup and that I often forget to shave my own legs.

I wish I could sleep.

I texted Lucy. She told me that I'm beautiful and to stop being ridiculous. She also moaned at me for bailing at the party, and when I told her that G and I had got together, she squealed and said *'finally'* as if she'd known all along. Were we really that obvious?

I love Lucy. Starting tomorrow, I'm going to be more like her—more Zen, less stressed. She's been a star for ages, was born into it. Her house in Los Angeles isn't far from mine but it's ten times bigger. The irony is that everyone takes me for the big-name star and treats her like a has-been, when she's everything I wish I could be.

She name-drops constantly. She doesn't mean to, but her life is one big party and it's always with her posse of famous friends. She never married, never had kids. I'm guessing she must be in her forties, at least — although you never know with actresses. Sometimes they get surgery in advance, before the wrinkles and sags even appear.

Someone's always having drama, and Lucy's always fixing it. She's kind of the person you want to be when you grow up, especially in my business.

I need to add 'Chill out' to my vision board. I'll do that then I'm going to sleep.

Nails, then vision board, then sleep. Promise.

* * * *

5 p.m.

I convinced G to book a hotel for the night so we could make love before we spend weeks at his parents' home. He didn't put up much of a fight.

I booked a room with a view, but I wasn't expecting a three-hundred-sixty-degree view. There are windows everywhere you look, from floor to ceiling, from the living room through to the bedroom. Even the small bathroom had a stunning view. The birds gliding past the windows are going to get a personal panorama of our first time.

"What is this place?" G stands there, his grubby messenger bag in hand, not quite knowing where to put it down. "It feels expensive."

I chuckle. "A private suite. I have a thing with this chain of hotels. Shit!" I've forgotten to do the whole story thing on my arrival. I quickly film a jumpy Boomerang of me saying *'Yay'* in front of the window and post it. "Remind me to film every single thing we do." *#poshhotel. #freeloaders.*

He raises his eyebrows. "Everything?"

"Well, I won't post it, but we can still film it if you'd like." His jaw drops. "I'm kidding. Are you serious? All it needs is for me to be hacked and the whole world would catch sight of your ample cock. Twitter would collapse under the weight of the thirst tweets."

"Aww. You think my dick is big. That's so sweet."

I can't think of a witty reply, so I resort to an exaggerated eye-roll.

"Where are we going to do it first?" I look around for somewhere that has at least a tiny bit of privacy then give up and throw myself onto the king-size bed.

"I feel so pressured to perform." He grins and looks me up and down as I undress on the bed, biting his lip. "Ugh. I've got stories to do, but I'll be right with you."

He posts a snap of the room, then sits down and films his daily motivational speech for his followers. He thinks he's some kind of spiritual lifestyle guru — or at least his fans do. I don't go in for all that. The only spirits I have in my life are the ones that come in a bottle.

I get bored in seconds and parade around naked in front of him and the birds while he extolls the virtues of Tolle. Eventually, my tits win, and he is motivated to extol my virtues instead.

* * * *

6 p.m.

They say Hollywood is sleazy, and they're not wrong. That actress, the one who taught me how to do blow jobs? She wasn't doing me a favor. She was preparing me for the casting couch.

You might think that the casting couch doesn't exist anymore but, my God, it does. Lucky for me, people exposing jerks on the Internet and the Me Too movement exist as well. Just as I was getting to an age where men in the film industry were ready to take advantage of me, they were stopped in their tracks by the thousands of women going public on their asses.

What does that mean for me? It means that the men that I worked with from the age of fifteen until, well, now, were terrified of initiating any kind of physical contact, warranted or not. And, as my life revolves around my work, my sex life had come to a grinding halt. Let's be honest... It had never really got off the ground to start with.

All this to say that G gave me an orgasm — several actual, real orgasms, like the ones you see in movies or porn. Although, I'm pretty sure neither are actually as real as the ones I just had.

Afterward, he fell asleep, his arms wrapped tightly around me. I was floating on air. Bits of me still tingled, waves waved, blood pumped...hard.

He'd started so gently, asking me questions every step of the way as he'd explored my body.

His lips had brushed my inner thigh. "Are you into any kinky stuff, BDSM, butt stuff?"

Uh. "No." At least I didn't think I was. *Probably no.* "I don't know. Are you?"

"No idea," he'd said, lifting his head from between my thighs and smiling at me, like a mechanic about to tell you what's wrong with your car. "I've never tried. You're not a virgin, are you? I don't mind. I mean, it's not a problem."

I giggled. "No."

He shrugged and went back to what he was doing. "You had me worried for a second. I would have taken it much more slowly. What positions make you come. What does it for you?"

"None." I bit my lip and looked away.

"None?" He popped his head back up again, looking like it was the saddest thing he'd ever heard. "Never?"

"None." I couldn't be sure I'd ever had an orgasm — not a proper real one, like you saw on the Internet.

He'd circled my clitoris with his thumb, slowly inserted one finger inside me, then two. I did like that, I told him, through my gasps.

Delighting in the fact that he would be the first man to give me an orgasm, he promised me that he would take his time. Bless his heart, I came in under a minute. It'd been a twenty-one-year wait, and he was a maestro with his hands.

So good. *Oh my God.* So, so good.

Sex is longer than I remember from the past and yet shorter than I imagined good sex would be — maybe ten, fifteen minutes. It had been a while, he explained, and I had been teasing him with all those sex scenes for months. And, he said, just the memory of that blow job was enough to make him want to come.

I feel beautiful and empowered and sexual.

I'm falling deeper than I imagined I could for G, and it's not what I had planned. Maybe France will clear things up, let us know where we stand. And maybe some more sex and orgasms too. That should definitely do the trick.

Chapter Five

August 5, 1 a.m.

We had the talk. The 'where are we going with this?' talk. Actually, no that's not true. G talked a lot, and I listened — and nodded and held back the tears.

G has told his parents that I'm his *'friend.'* He didn't know what we are, or how I feel about him. It's all too new to be putting labels on things — or so he says.

He reminded me that sometimes actors get together during or after a film, but it's because of the forced proximity and that maybe we won't feel that way in a week.

He's so sweet, but my heart started breaking into little pieces as he was saying it, because I totally don't feel like I deserve this amazing guy who thinks about other people's feelings and is in control of his emotions.

I cried a blubbery, snotty cry, and he held me and reassured me that everything was fine and that he wasn't saying we aren't going to fall in love. Now I can't sleep and I think I finished all the little bottles in the minibar.

* * * *

10:15 a.m.

G woke me up at some ungodly hour, like 8 a.m. or something equally horrendous. We fooled around, then he went down to the gym. We were packed and checked out by ten.

There should be some hiatus rule that means I don't have to get up early for at least a month. My body needs sleep. *All the sleep.*

Being driven by G is enlightening. He has such a peaceful nature, and he's a really good driver. He hasn't sworn at anybody, not even when a guy cut him off on the freeway. Admittedly, I'm orgasm-based biased, but he emits a kind of calm around him wherever he goes. It's very soothing.

I cursed under my breath, though, because people can't get away with cutting other people off and not be cursed at.

It's not like I've got any experience when it comes to driving. I never got my license. People have been driving me places ever since other people started paying them to do it, and it has never occurred to me that I might want to drive one day.

"Do you want to listen to some music or a podcast? Grab my phone."

I rifle around in the famous messenger bag at my feet. I expect to find a treasure map, maybe some old, leather-bound books, a compass and a few ancient artifacts. Instead, it's his wallet, his phone, some spare underwear and his journal. *Tragically disappointing.*

"What's your password?" I ask.

"123456." *What the fuck?*

"Seriously? Aren't you afraid of people getting into your stuff?" He has no sense of fame, no wariness when it comes to his fans. Shit, I've got a password—one of those swipey-line things—and my phone takes a photo of anybody daring to go any further.

"I've got nothing to hide. Why? What's on your phone?"

"Photos, thoughts, links to fan fiction." I don't have nudes—I'm not stupid—but I do have private stuff on there that I don't want to share.

"You read fan fiction?" He pauses. "Shee, do you read fan fiction about yourself?"

Gulp. There's no shame in that, right?

"If someone wrote a book about you, you'd want to read it. Well, not you, but…like a version of you."

"Of course."

Is he judging me right now? I'd been in a popular teen show for three years. There are a ton of ships with my character's name in them. It's thrilling to see how people write about me, how much people still love my character.

"You should read *Love in the Name of Parcus*. It's a fucking classic." 'Parcus' is my ship name, Polly and Marcus.

There are T-shirts and computer stickers.

I might own those T-shirts and computer stickers.

"And you don't mind people writing stuff like that about you?"

That *definitely* sounds a little judgy.

"Well, it's not me, is it? Some of it is beautiful. People believe so much in these characters. They need them to live on. I think that means I've done my job, as an actor, if they want it so much."

He turns to me and grins before looking back at the road. There's a genuine sense of admiration coming from that smile. "You love what you do. I knew it when they did the chemistry test. Every word, every nuance... You're so good at it."

"It's all I've ever known. I can't do anything else. I have to be good at it." *Did that sound as tragic when it came out of my mouth as it did when it popped into my head? I fucking hope not.*

"We all have the potential to be anything we want."

Yeah, right. If we look and sound like you, we do.

"Is that from one of your books?" I ask.

He laughs. "No. That's me saying that the possibilities in life are endless. I think you're incredible, Shee — funny, sexy, smart. You can do whatever you put your mind to."

If only he knew how hard I work at looking like I do. I'm not naturally sporty. This body is a combination of having to forego anything resembling tasty food and having to force myself to go to the gym every single fucking day of my life.

"I am very few of those things. I didn't finish school. I burn pasta. I have absolutely no idea how to repair things or do anything except learn my lines, stand in the right place and occasionally look pretty with the help of a dozen stylists and make-up artists. I *am* pretty sexy, though. A fucking love machine, that's me." This makes him laugh even louder, which is flattering, you know, because it's funny, but, at the same time, there's nothing funny about this fucking love machine.

Note to self—never again refer to yourself as a 'fucking love machine'.

Never. It's weird.

"There's so much more to you than you know. You write. I've seen you scribbling away in the journal I gave you." Oh God, imagine if he reads it?

"Those are my private thoughts. Ninety-percent of it is me talking about your dick."

He puts his hand over his cock. "I am not a penis. I am a man. I have feelings and emotions."

"Sometimes I write about what you do with your fingers too."

He chuckles, shaking his head at me in despair. "Are you ever going to choose some music or are we going to spend the rest of the journey discussing my body? No, don't answer that. Just choose some music."

I can discuss G's body all day if he wants me to, but I opt for a playlist and imagining him naked instead. I giggle at my dirty thoughts and concentrate on being an attentive girlfriend. "Tell me about the book you're reading—the one you keep telling your followers about."

G comes alive when he talks Tolle, like an English teacher talking about Shakespeare—the type that gets enthused about classic books that they make you read in school and talks about them endlessly. G reads a book, then reads it again, highlights it then evaluates it. He quotes it constantly and uses the knowledge that he has gained from it, but in a reasoned way.

He really isn't just a penis. I fell in love with his brain first.

Feeling so inadequate all the time and meeting someone who wants to be so aware of their life sends chills down my spine—and not in a good way. G's confidence and ability to evaluate everything scares me.

One day he is going to wake up and re-read, highlight and evaluate me, and find out that there is nothing in me that he needs.

He seeks a greater meaning in life, while appreciating every second of the present—or so he'd said in his latest Insta caption.

I grip onto each day, holding on by the very tips of my fingers.

Chapter Six

We've booked first class, but, at G's request, we don't do the famous people thing where we get dropped off at a separate entrance and go through special security. "I don't like all that stuff," he says, "acting like we're different or special." The thing is, though, that we are.

So, we queue…and queue…and queue some more.

"See? It isn't so bad." He smiles through gritted teeth. God forbid a man should ever admit that he's wrong.

The paps have followed us through the airport. I didn't even call them, and I know G wouldn't have. I suspect Suzy is squeezing the final drops of money out of me before my hiatus. News of our coupleness will be imminent. Well, obviously we know, but the rest of the world is about to learn about us, too.

The man behind me pushes up against my back and the screaming child in his arms slowly runs her sticky fingers down my hair. "I hate you," I whisper to G.

"No, you don't. This is good for you. It grounds you a little." Oh, something is definitely grinding me. I turn and give the man behind me a dirty glance. He has his kid in his arms, for fuck's sake.

Luckily the actual flight is calmer — only three selfies and an autograph.

I film G sleeping with his mouth open and post it on TikTok. *Revenge is sweet.*

* * * *

August 6, 2 p.m. French time

His dad, Bob, picks us up at the airport. Clearly thrilled to see his son, he has a grin as wide as his face for the entire journey home. The two-hour drive is via the steepest roads in France and up the highest mountains — or so it feels. I'm a city girl. I don't really do mountains. There aren't as many beaches as I'd pictured. In fact, none at all.

The family home is a big farm at the end of a dusty road. There are four or five stone outbuildings, and a lovely farmhouse decked in flowers, slap bang at the end of the driveway.

Picture perfect.

G lights up when he sees his family. They are all standing outside awaiting our arrival with arms wide open and huge grins on their faces. Linda, his mom and, *oh God, I've forgotten all their names already. Madison? Mackenzie?* One of them definitely starts with an M.

We step onto the porch and are set upon by hugs upon hugs, like a massive pile-on of arms and chests. I stand back and let the family octopus finish its feeding frenzy before going in for a handshake and a 'hello'.

Then we're ushered out back for a grill and a buffet. There's so much food. His mother, to put it lightly, is efficient as fuck. She has to be, though, having brought up four kids while running a farm. Everybody is present, even a couple of grandchildren. It is overwhelming and ever-so-slightly suffocating.

They are all so different. G is the youngest and the mirror image of his dad. The other children all take after their mom's side. His parents are both what my grandma would have referred to as 'hippies'. I guess these days we say 'boho chic'. Caftans and tie-dye shirts abound. A faint hint of patchouli oil hangs in the air, wafted around by the wind chimes.

"You're really close to your family," I say to him. I've never seen a group of people so happy to be around each other. It makes me very uncomfortable.

"Yeah. Why does that surprise you?"

"You seem artistic, tortured. I expected a little hardship or something, but this is the 'Little House on the fucking Prairie'." I'm talking quietly but I see his eyes widen as I swear. *Shit.* I'm not used to having to tame my language. I bite my tongue.

He grins and shakes his head. "I can see why you get that vibe. Trust me. We're not perfect. I love these guys, but don't be fooled. We don't always get along." He takes my hand in his. "Is your family not the same?"

"I have one older sister. I'm the baby, like you." I shrug my shoulders. "We get along okay. We're not really close or anything, but we don't hate each other, either. I haven't lived at home since I was fourteen, and even then, my parents were at work all the time, and I spent my evenings in acting class or singing lessons or whatever else my grandma signed me up for."

Grandma was the driving force behind my career. Obsessed with pageants, she'd forced my mom to enter all kinds of talent shows and 'Miss This' and 'Miss That'. When I was born, it was my turn. I still have a pile of trophies somewhere in a closet.

My sister was what my grandma referred to as 'not really pageant material', which was her way of saying that neither her talent nor her looks were good enough. That drove a wedge between us that has never been fixed. She doesn't hate me for it, but she resents the attention I'd gotten — as if any of it is my fault.

My mom refused to give up her high paid executive position when she had kids — understandable in so many ways — but it meant we spent our childhoods being dragged from one pageant to the other and supposedly being home-schooled by Grandma. My sister would read schoolbooks at the back of the room, and I would perform for the crowds — until the day I was spotted by a talent agent and Grandma's dreams came true.

"Is that why you never go home?"

If you could call it that. Home is my house in LA, currently sitting empty, waiting patiently for my return so I can empty out the dead plants from their pots and throw the sour milk away. The household I grew up in never welcomed me as this family has done today, even when I'd lived there. That was never home.

"I suppose so. We keep in touch with FaceTime and phone calls. I guess they don't miss me as much as your family clearly misses you." They don't miss me at all.

In fact, I haven't even told them I'm here. Grandma is gone now. There's nobody left to care.

"My family only miss the extra pair of hands to help with the outdoor work," he says.

Is he reassuring me? That's G down to the bone. Always a hand on my back to remind me that he's there for me, a gentle word to comfort me. It isn't true, though. They'd showered him with love when we'd arrived.

It's getting harder and harder to remind myself that I am just his 'friend.' I haven't even earned the word 'girl' in front of it. That is as low on the scale as you can get for someone you are actively having sex with.

Bob walks past and plonks another hamburger onto my plate. "Eat up. There's plenty more where that came from."

I'm going to weigh twenty pounds more by the end of this trip. Thank God for filters. A couple of taps on the screen and none of my followers will know. One day my hiatus will be over, and I am going to need every one of those fans.

Popularity is everything. The pap pics at the airport have brought fresh blood to my Insta, and I am as determined as I can to keep them. "*You are nothing without fans*," Suzy often reminds me. I should get that put on a T-shirt.

"So, you're G's friend," says his mother, biting into a veggie burger. "Tell us about you," she adds, munching away.

"Mom," says G's sister, cringing from embarrassment, "everybody knows who she is." She winks at me. "She's, like, super famous."

She chuckles and swallows her mouthful. "Well, I don't know. Are you on the TV? You're not one of those TikTak people are you, with the dancing?"

"It's 'Tok', and Shee is an actress, Mom," injects G, who is trying to balance a plate, a beer and a wriggling nephew in his arms.

"Are you in *The Avengers*? The grands love *The Avengers*, don't they, honey?" She nudges her husband, who is digging into his food and not listening to one word of the conversation.

He nods and carries on eating. He looks like he agrees with his wife a lot. Probably how he ended up with so many children.

I give a friendly smile. "I'm afraid I'm not one of *The Avengers*. Sorry. I was in quite a few teen movies and a TV series, but more for a younger generation." I glance over at G. Was that rude?

"Is that how you know our Guillaume?" It's the first time I've ever heard someone use his full name, and it throws me.

"No, uh." I turn to 'Gee-yome' and throw him a 'why have you never mentioned me before?' look. His mother doesn't know that we work together. I've never come up in conversation?

He has the dignity to blush. "Mom, she's my co-star. We just made a movie together. The big one."

His mother narrows her eyes. "Ah." Does she know how many love scenes were in that film? Is she calculating how many times I'd cavorted, almost naked, with her son? She smiles and I breathe again. "The sex one, huh? That's nice." *Fuck.*

Luckily the conversation quickly turns to the subject of the farm. I stand there, nodding and eating, joining in as much as I can for someone who is completely out of my time and comfort zone. It looks like G will be called on to do all kinds of important jobs over the next few days, and I'll be needed to help set up for his dad's fiftieth birthday party.

"You're only fifty?" I say it without thinking. I am really going to have to invest in some kind of mute button for my mouth if I want to avoid offending anybody else during my stay. "Sorry... That came out wrong. Of course, you look fifty, younger even. I meant that you all have these grown-up children. I, um... You're so young."

His father smiles at me, the creases in his eyes crinkling with amusement at my embarrassment. He is an outdoor man...weathered. It is easy to see why I would make the error of adding another ten years to his age. "People where we come from get married young, and my wife and I are a fine example. High School sweethearts, we got hitched at eighteen. This big guy arrived a year later." He taps his eldest son, Thibault, on the shoulder. It's pronounced 'Tee-bo'. I'd called him 'T-Bone' several times before someone had finally corrected me. "Then we had the twins, then this little dude came along twenty-two years ago. Such a blessing, all of them." He takes his wife's hand in his and shakes it a little.

The way they look at each other. *So much love in this household.*

Romantic gestures in my house were kept to a strict minimum. My parents hardly spoke. They sat glued to the TV every evening, then bed at nine because they had to be up at six. I couldn't remember a single time my mom ever held my dad's hand.

It's not that I don't like it. I'm happy for G, but it is another nail in the coffin for our future if he wants this from me.

I've never been very good at the touchy-feely sweet romantic stuff.

Maybe he can teach me.

After lunch, G suggests that we go for a walk. All the chit-chat has been hard with jet-lag and trying to remember everybody's names. A bit of alone time, just the two of us, would be good.

"Be back before sunset," his mom says. "You have chores to do this evening." How big is this place that we'll be out for hours? I know farms can go on for miles, but I don't know if I'm in the mood to do a tour of one. I'm more in the mood for a nap and some canoodling in the afternoon sun.

We change into jeans and sneakers. G's demeanor changes, too—like when a snake sheds its skin. He takes off his city-boy persona, and with the comfier clothes comes a freer attitude. He's almost skipping along the dusty road as we follow the farm dogs toward open fields.

It reassures me. If he can be so comfortable, then so can I, eventually. The freedom this place gives is already starting to rub off on me.

He takes me off-road, up a small path and through a wooded area. The afternoon sun is sweltering. We lie down next to each other in the shade of a tree and make out like teenagers, under the clothes, over the bra.

I squint at the sky. "I don't like people touching me and yet we're here and all I want is to feel your hands on my body."

"I noticed. You flinched when my brother hugged you." He pauses. "You don't do relationships, do you?

I've known you, what? Three, four months? In that whole time, you've never mentioned a best friend or even a close one. Everybody you talk about is either someone you once worked with or someone you're working with now."

Harsh...but true.

"I've never really thought about it. I had a best friend growing up. Becky. We played around each other's houses and rode our bikes around the block." Last I knew, Becky was working in real estate, but that was, what? Three years ago? *Three years. Wow.*

"Is there a reason why you don't like people touching you? Did, uh, did something happen?" He threads his fingers through mine and rolls onto his side. "You can tell me."

I scrunch up my nose. Talking about the 'whys' is hard. "Nothing sinister there. I like my personal space. My parents aren't really huggers — nor is my sister. I do spend most of my life nervously awaiting the next non-consensual hug from a stranger."

He frowns as if I'd said something completely ridiculous. "Strange men hug you? I've never noticed that."

Wow. You literally saved me from one the other day, but whatever...

"Don't strange women hug you? I bet your fans are all touchy-feely," I ask. God, if I was one of his fans and I bumped into him in the street, I'd find it hard not to at least cop a little bicep feel.

I'm such a fucking hypocrite.

His eyes widen, shocked at the suggestion that any one of his fans would be so rude. "No, and I make sure I never touch anybody who wants a selfie." If it were any other man, I'd suspect foul play, but G is gold.

I pluck at a blade of grass, tear it in two, throw it in the air to float away in the breeze. "Men put their arms around me all the time. I'm small, and they feel like they know me. You'll see it, now that I've mentioned it. Every time we meet new people — or at least people new to me — the men will put their arm around me and pull me into their chest. It's not necessarily sexual, but it's very intimidating."

I'm not tall. One of the first things most people say when they met me is 'you look taller on the screen'. It seems to encourage men to take on a completely unwarranted protective stance. A hand will creep over my shoulder, like in the cinema on a first date, then the little neck hug to pull me closer. A chill goes down my spine. *Ugh.* I hate it.

His hand, still linked through mine, grasps me tighter. "I had no idea. Why don't you tell them? No, don't answer that. They'll call you a frigid whore."

"Exactly."

He poses his head on his hand, leaning forward just enough to let me feel the warmth of his breath on my face. "Do I reassure you?"

I pick at the grass again, disturbing a bee. We watch him buzz around us until he's sure we aren't flowers. "You terrify me."

He laughs, coyly, as if he's waiting for the punchline. But there isn't one. "I terrify you?"

"Of course you do. You're the anti-me, my polar opposite. Your shit is so together that it's positively forming diamonds."

That earns a louder laugh and a hint of indignation. "I'm not so sure that's true. And why does that scare you, the idea of me having my shit together?"

"Because one day you're going to wake up and see that I am never going to change. I'm not going to suddenly do housework or be any good at grown-up stuff. I'm always going to be down to my last pair of panties, and we are always going to be out of milk."

He sits up, crosses his legs underneath him and pulls me up too. "Shee, how many calories was your lunch?"

"Over two thousand." *What? It's been a long day. There have been grilled hamburgers and curly fries. I'll get right back on the diet tomorrow.*

He picks a little yellow flower and sticks it behind my ear. "Recite one of my lines from our movie?"

I think about it for a few seconds. One of his lines? *"Umm…I want to go back to that moonlit beach in Maui and kiss her all over again."*

He claps down with his hands on my shoulders, almost shaking me. "You see? You weren't even in that scene."

"So?"

He throws his head back in frustration. "Shee, it's not that you're not organized or that you haven't got your shit together. It's that you have different priorities than me. You've been so focused on being an actor that it's all you know how to do." He pauses, scrunches up his nose. *Is he wondering if he has offended me?* "Which is great, because you are one amazing actor."

He isn't wrong. My personal life might be a disaster, but my career has always been a huge success. "I never saw it like that."

Pulling me into a hug, he holds me tight against his body, next to his heart. "That's because you don't see yourself as I do. You define yourself by what you think others want, or what you think I want. You can't even see how incredible you are."

Have I lost all sense of my own worth? If acting is the only thing I can do, has it become who I am — and the only thing that I am? He grabs my head in his hands, looks my face up and down and kisses me on the lips. "What terrifies me the most about being with you is that you are so fucking awesome, and you don't even know it. Someone is going to steal you away from me."

I balk, pull my head back and look him straight in the eyes. "Never." The mere idea of betraying him is just ridiculous.

"Never say never. Nobody's perfect."

He is, though, lying here in the grass, with the bees and the flowers and his big strong hands. He is all I could want.

"Cross my heart." The heart that aches to be more to him than a passing fling. The heart that stutters every time I remember that we're just friends.

There are a million and one things we need to do — unpack, shower. His family must be wondering where the hell we are, but we lay out on that patch of grass for what feels like hours. We speak little, kiss a lot. We sleep. We cuddle. There's tranquility to being here, and I never want it to end.

Chapter Seven

August 7, 6 a.m.

We are woken at some ungodly hour by G's mom. Breakfast will be on the table in half an hour, then we're expected to help with the day's business. No, actually that's a lie. We were woken at 5 a.m. by a fucking rooster who'd decided to tell us the sun was coming out. Then what sounded like hundreds of starving farm dogs decided it was time for breakfast—and that woke the donkey.

They go '*Cocorico*' in France, apparently. Roosters, not dogs or donkeys. It didn't sound any different to me.

Oh, and here they call them 'coqs'. Lol.

The room we're in, an attic room right at the top of the house, is swelteringly hot. For the first time in my life, I know how a ball sac feels in a jockstrap. My sweat has sweat. This does not bode well for the day ahead. I've hardly slept, for mainly sexual reasons, and now

I'm expected to be sociable and helpful too in this searing heat.

"Can you switch on the air conditioning? I'm literally melting."

He takes in a deep breath. "This is France. They don't do air conditioning here."

"What?" You have to be kidding. "Really?"

"Well, that's not entirely true. If you go to the south, by the coast, they do, but this is the countryside. We close the blinds during the days and let the night breeze cool us as we sleep." He shrugs and gets out of bed. "Come on. Let's get showered and ready. You can meet the animals and enjoy a little mountain breeze. We have chores."

I've been promised a getaway, but it feels like even here everybody wants a piece of me, too. "Chores? I didn't sign up for early mornings and farm work."

"Go back to sleep then." The smile on his mouth does not correspond with the irritation in his voice.

I cave and throw him a radiant smile. "I'm sorry. I'm jetlagged and hot and tired. I'll be better after a coffee and a shower."

My grandma's words echo through my mind. Before every audition she'd crouch down and whisper, "You're special, not like everybody else. You have to smile and look good all the time so people can see how special you are." I still do it. I still smile for the people, on and offline. Everybody gets the cheerful Sophie that they expect.

I don't feel special at 6 a.m., though, no matter how hard I work at it. I feel like death warmed up.

After dragging ourselves out of bed, into the shower and down to the kitchen table where breakfast is served, we both at least look a little more human, even if we aren't quite feeling it yet.

I'm lying, of course, because G always looks attractive as hell, even after a sleepless night. It is a gift not bestowed upon many, and I am totally jealous of it. But he looks even hotter after a shower, and there's added perfume.

His family acknowledges us, barely, as they tuck into the hearty meal G's mother has laid out—ham, cheese, fresh bread, endless choices of jellies and jams. I'm not sure what work we're going to do, but if this is the sustenance required to do it, I am probably going to break a nail and a sweat.

"Sophie, would you mind helping out on the farm today?" asks Thibault. "Dad and I have got to go see about that camel in Auvergne."

"Camel?" I ask.

"Yes," replies G's brother. "There's an animal sanctuary not far from here who contacted us about a camel they rescued. We're going to see if she'll be a good fit."

"So, this is more like a zoo than a farm?" I'd heard them talking about it last night, but I still thought it was just your regular farm animals. Camels are a whole other thing.

G puts a hand over mine, grasping my fingers. "This is what they call a *ferme pedagogique*, like a mini-zoo. We've got all the normal farm animals you'd expect and there's the llamas, the alpacas and, apparently, now maybe a camel."

His family explains, while talking over each other, that G's dad had inherited the farm from his French grandparents, and they had sold their home and belongings in Idaho on a whim and flown over on the next plane, cases in hand, to set up this business.

"All the kids were grown except Guillaume, so it seemed like something we could do," says, Linda, clearing plates away as she speaks. "Then one by one, they all moved over here too." She ruffles her youngest grandson's hair. "And we're all the better for it."

"So, what do you want us to do today?" asks G. His dad hands him a long, handwritten list of chores and he studies it, taking his hand away from mine and rubbing his hand across his abs as he reads. He arches his back, blinks through the tiredness and yawns. I can't take my eyes off him.

I've seen him do that a million times, but now he's mine. He catches me staring out of the corner of his eye and turns, winking at me.

Bob points at the list. "The twins will deal with the tourists. We need you to give the llamas their vitamins, including Tornado, clean out the pigs and the chickens, repair the goat fence, and —"

"Tornado needs a vitamin?" asks G, his eyes wide. "Can't we put it in his water?"

His father roars with laughter. "Send in Sophie. He's always nicer to the ladies."

I shake my head. "Why do I feel like I'm going to die by llama today?"

"You'll be fine," says Linda, placing her hands on my shoulders. "My Guillaume knows what he's doing. He spent enough summers helping to run the place."

I look up at her. "I bet you have so many stories to share."

"Oh, so many," she replies, smiling, "but now's not the time. Go on. You've all got work to do, and I have a party to prepare."

G takes me out back to the mudroom and hands me the stinkiest old pair of rubber boots and a bandana.

"You're going to need these."

"It's as dry as a bone out there."

"Not in the pig enclosure it's not," he replies, handing me a shovel. "What we're going to be shoveling is not dry at all. The bandana is for your hair. All the staff wear them. It helps the visitors find us." *Eww*, the mere idea of scooping up poop all day makes me want to fly back to that air-conditioned suite at the hotel with all the windows.

I tie the scarf around my hair and follow him as he pushes a wheelbarrow to our first destination of the day.

When in Rome, I guess.

The farm is beautifully landscaped, with a wooden decking path taking you from one enclosure to the next. The place is huge, and the animals have enough space to enjoy their lives. As farm animals go, they don't have an unhappy life. There's no chance of landing on someone's plate, and they have a comfy, safe enclosure and all the leftovers they can handle.

"We bring money and visitors to the village, even though we're a little way out, so they give us all of their food scraps from the local restaurant. These guys get the best organic vegetables," says G, as he unlocks the gate. "Come meet our little friends. Guys, this is Shee-Shee." He holds out his hand as if to introduce us. "Shee, this is Marcel, René and Lucien."

To my shock and surprise, pigs are cute. They aren't big and smelly. They are average-sized and kind of hairy, with little round bellies.

"Can I pet them?"

"Sure," he replies, holding my hand and pulling me closer to them. I crouch down and scratch the smallest one behind the ear. He kind of leans into it and moves his head around so that I get all the other bits that need a good scratch.

"Well, you are adorable." They honestly don't smell that bad. The straw in their enclosure has kind of absorbed the icky stuff and it really isn't as disgusting as I'd imagined. "Shall we get your home all clean?" I reluctantly move away from my little piggy friend and grab my tools.

Shoveling shit, as it turns out, is quite an enjoyable thing to do with your boyfriend. I mean, let's be honest. Lying on a beach is great for a holiday, but everybody does that. We swap stories about pets and animals in general, slip and slide on the yuckiest stuff and get the three little piggies' home all spick and span.

I can't say the same for the chickens, however.

Creepy-looking, spiky-beaked avian monsters from hell, these guys are not happy with our presence in their home. Their poop smells like it comes from the bowels of the deep.

"I don't think" —*heave*—"I can do this" —*heave*. I stick my bandana over my nose and go in for another try. *Heave. Nope.* I and my shovel retreat, and we stand back to watch G do his thing.

Next on the list is the llama enclosure.

"Llamas and alpacas are generally quite docile animals. These guys are used to seeing the public every day, and they grew up here, so they're happy to let people in the pen." He opens the gate. "This is the fun part of the day."

Giant fluffy teddy bears. No word of a lie that these guys are big and soft—and fluffy and cute. Okay, so they smell a bit like week-old socks and, you know, there's still poop everywhere and stuff, but they are *so* cute. They have big old buck teeth and jaws that wibble and wobble from side to side when you give them a carrot, and their ears kind of flop and fly in all directions. We stick the vitamins into carrots and feed them to them by hand.

"I don't know what you were worried about. They're fine."

"Oh, this isn't the enclosure with Tornado." G turns and points to the next field along, where a lone, evil-looking llama stands high on a rock, lording over every other animal in the park. "That's Tornado."

A shiver goes down my spine. "And he has to have a vitamin?"

"Yup."

Tornado turns to look at us, as if he knows and as if our days are now numbered. "Holy crap." I gulp. "He's staring right at me, and I can't look away."

We give the Brady Bunch another quick hug and step out of the enclosure toward certain death. "He's not dangerous. He's just not very friendly. You'll be fine."

"I'm what? Me? No way. No thank you, sir. Nope."

G hands me the bucket. "My dad wasn't kidding when he said Tornado prefers women. He really does. You'll be fine. I swear."

I can do this, right? He's just a llama. I open the gate and step in. Tornado glances down from his rock. "You going to come down here, fella?" I shake the carrot bucket and his ears perk up, but he doesn't move an inch. "I'm going to have to climb up," I say to G, gesticulating at the rock.

"Be careful," he replies, giving me a thumbs up, as if that's going to save me from a rabid llama kick if everything goes wrong.

"Hey, fella, all I'm going to do is come up to your rock and give you a carrot." I've read that lowering the tone of your voice and speaking slowly can help in difficult situations. I have no idea if that works in encounters with animals named after natural disasters.

Tornado turns to look at me, his beady-eyed grimace daring me to take a step farther. I hold out the vitamin-filled carrot and try desperately to steady my trembling hand.

I did not sign up for this when I agreed to come to this place. So far, the rolling in the hay and midnight assignations under the French stars have been very limited, and my trip has mostly involved hippies and chicken-shit. This is not the romantic trip to France I was promised.

I proffer the carrot once more, but he doesn't budge.

"You've got this!" shouts G from thirty feet away. *Are you sure? Are you sure I've 'got this'?* Nothing feels very 'got'.

I advance a couple of more steps, and Tornado does a kind of heaving noise — the same thing I'd done in the chicken shed — and sways back and forth.

Not dissimilar to that scene in *The Exorcist*, he throws back his head and sprays me with a liquid that smells like three-week-old rotten lasagna.

"Shee," says G, sidling up ever-so-slowly to the fence beneath Tornado's favorite rock.

"Yes," I reply, as llama juice drips from my every pore.

"Run!"

I back away as fast as I can, leap off the rock and turn to find the nearest exit. But llamas are quick—like *way* quick—and my only solution is to jump the fence into the next enclosure. Goats run in all directions as I barrel into their home, slipping on something sticky and landing on my butt with an almighty splat into a pile of wet droppings.

Tornado stops in his tracks a couple of meters from the fence, saunters over, warily, to inspect the damage he has caused, lowers his head and grabs the carrot out of my hand. He munches his spoils, smugly lording over me in victory, then saunters back off to his rock.

"Oh my God, are you okay?" G lifts me to my feet and inspects my soiled jeans. "Let's get you back to the house and cleaned up. It's almost lunchtime, anyway."

I look down at my clothes, smothered in all kinds of dark, smelly liquids, and try, in vain, to wipe some of them off. "If that was how Tornado reacts to women, I can't even imagine what he does to men."

G cringes, and chuckles at my sarcasm. "He has never hurt anybody. He just doesn't like humans very much."

Pain sears up my butt. "I think I broke my coccyx."

"Do you need me to rub some cream in there? I've got just the thing." He winks at me and bites his lip, just at the idea, gently placing a hand on my posterior and giving it a rub.

"You're hilarious." I stumble out of the goat enclosure, put an arm over his shoulder, and head, slowly, back to the house. If the sight of me like this doesn't put him off, then pretty much nothing will. Despite his protestations, he might be falling for me after all.

Linda has prepared a lovely picnic, to be enjoyed under the midday sun. Once I've showered all the goat feces out of my hair and put on something a little less stinky, we grab a blanket and head for our favorite clearing in the woods.

G helps himself to a sandwich, plonks down onto the ground and taps the grass next to him. "Sit down."

"I can't. My butt feels like it's gone ten rounds with a heavyweight boxer and it lost."

He throws me a sympathetic smile. "I'm sorry about today. I thought you'd enjoy it. I forgot how much work all this stuff takes. It has been a while."

"Do they expect you to work here one day? You seem pretty good at it." He seems perfectly at home both in the city in a suit and here in torn jeans and a grubby T-shirt.

"No." He laughs, shaking his head. "I'm terrible at it. You're just so bad that you make me look good for once."

I grab a sandwich and lean up against a tree. "Well, I did make some llama friends, so it isn't all terrible. It is beautiful here, though..." I look over at the mountains surrounding us. "That makes up for all the chicken shit and goat poop." He taps the blanket beside him again, wanting me to move closer. I crouch down, knees bent, my butt floating a few inches off the ground.

"It is," he replies. "I always forget. Then when I get back and step out of my car, breathe the fresh, clean French air and look around me, it all comes back. Serenity."

"Will you come back here one day?"

"To live? No. This part of my life is over. It stays with me, but I've moved on. I have big plans, and they don't involve deranged llamas, fortunately."

"Do they involve me?" A blush heats my cheeks. I didn't mean to say it. It sort of slipped out of my mouth. But that doesn't mean I'm not desperate to know if he's changed his mind.

"Tolle says to think about the present. Live for the moment. I know that kind of contradicts what I said, but relationships have always been difficult for me. I don't like to think about what will happen to us." He lifts his hand to my head and plays with my hair, tucking it behind my ear. "You're in my life now, and I'm grateful for that and for each special moment we share — even today, with your catastrophic introduction to farming." He is smiling as he says it. That isn't the answer that I wanted, but it isn't an outright no.

I nod and slide down next to him. "Okay." The silence between us as we finish our meal speaks volumes. He is too scared to make the next move, and I am too eager to fall in love.

"You see," he says as we stroll back to the house a couple of hours later. "You can do so much more than you thought. You're not 'just an actress'. You proved that, at least, today."

"I guess so." I don't doubt that I can do anything I put my mind to. I've simply never tried.

"And about what I said earlier... I work hard to be in the present, but I'm only human, and I sometimes think about things that happened to me in the past and what the future might hold. It scares me. That's why I'm teaching myself to live for now. But don't think for a minute that that doesn't mean I couldn't fall in love with you, Shee — or that I haven't already."

It might not be the declaration of eternal love I secretly desire but, for today, that's good enough for me, my sore butt and my sunburned nose.

Chapter Eight

August 7, 6 p.m.

Our reward for a hard day's work is a delicious meal, the most relaxing swim I've ever taken in my life, then drinks in front of the fire pit.

"Our Sophie here has a bright future ahead of her if she ever wants to go into farming," says G's dad, laughing, after hearing about my escapades in the goat enclosure. He has a gruff laugh, as if his voice has gone a bit rusty. He'd shouted a lot today, when they'd brought back their camel. I've seen him a couple of times with a cigar in his hand. It goes well with the look of an aging French farmer, slightly disheveled, tanned skin through to the bone and a hint of white stubble on his chin. His hair is the same as G's, but it is more salt and pepper.

Right now, he looks more like a kindly uncle. He's sat back in a rocking chair under the stars, sipping a beer and mocking my agricultural abilities.

"I might have to invest in a sturdier pair of pants," I reply, adjusting into my chair. My butt still hurts like I've been a very bad girl indeed — and yet, I've been so good.

"Who wants another beer?" asks G's brother, getting up.

"No, it's okay. I'll go," I say, grabbing the empties and heading toward the kitchen.

G's mom is busy baking something for tomorrow. I've never met anybody like Linda. She's constantly cooking and cleaning and serving people and never stops to do anything for herself.

There are two types of people among my friends, when it comes to cooking. I know people who own every single type of dish and machine — like the one where you put everything in a big pot and you come back three hours later and you have a gourmet meal for eight. And there are people like me. I own a bowl-shaped pan that doubles both as a saucepan and a frying pan and one wooden spoon. Even my cutlery and plates allow for only one extra guest.

"Beers are in the fridge at the back," she says, pointing to a small pantry at the far end of the kitchen. I replaced the empties, popping my head around the door to ask if she wants one. She shakes her head. She hasn't joined us for a drink since we arrived.

Linda is most definitely an entirely different species from me.

"What are you baking?" I ask as I walk back past her. "It smells delicious."

"Cookies and bread. Well, the cookies are baking, and the bread is rising. Do you want to try one?" She holds out a plate of warm chocolate chip deliciousness, and I dive in.

"Thank you. Do you not want to join us in the garden?" It must be so lonely being stuck in here all day. You'd have thought she'd want the company.

"And talk about goats and llamas all night? No thank you. I'm better off in my kitchen. I've got my radio on and I can take my time to gather my thoughts from the day." For somebody who spent most of the day alone doing one thing or another, she must have a hell of a lot of thoughts. "So, you're our G's new sweetheart, huh?"

"I suppose I am, yes." Am I allowed to say that? Is it even true? On one hand it has been made very clear to me that I'm just his 'friend', but we're sharing a bedroom. Linda isn't dumb. She has worked out that we're at least sleeping together.

"He's fragile, my boy. He's not had a lot of luck in love. But I'm sure you know that already."

All I know is what G had spoken about this afternoon. He isn't one for talking about past girlfriends. There was a long-term love in the past, but that's all I know. I nod anyway, not wanting Linda to think that my relationship with her son is based entirely on carnal pleasures, and for her to believe that we discuss stuff too.

"Of course, you'll meet Juliette this weekend, at the party, seeing as she's family."

I lean back against the kitchen counter, checking first that I don't get flour all over my butt. "Family?" *Oh my God.* "Like, a...cousin?"

She is taken aback by my shocked expression, before chuckling to herself when she realizes that I don't know what on earth she is talking about. "Oh gosh no, not like that. Juliette's family and my husband's family are very close. Our kids would all hang out when we visited. They're like family, but they're not actual family. Good lord, this isn't 'The North'."

The North of where?

"You should know," she says, leaning in and lowering her voice. "Bob and I have a very different take on relationships. We don't exactly subscribe to the idea of monogamy."

"But you've been married since forever, haven't you?"

"Yes, but we believe that sexuality is a liberal affair. That's part of the reason we moved to France. They're way more accepting of this kind of thing over here." *What kind of thing, exactly? Is she talking, affairs? Polyamory?* Whatever it is, this middle-aged woman in a bright orange kaftan, baking bread in her kitchen, does not look like she partakes of anything too daring. "And we encourage our children to embrace the idea of love being something that should be shared…freely."

Oh God, this definitely sounds like something I *don't* want to do. She smiles, claps the flour from her hands and gets back to her baking. The conversation is over.

I grab the beers and another cookie and head back outside.

"Thank you," says G, as I open a bottle and hand it to him. His family have gotten their guitars out and are belting out a rousing version of *Stand by Me*.

"I had a chat with your mom…in the kitchen." *He knows, right?* She'd said that they encourage their kids to be liberal and free too.

"Oh yeah?"

I lean forward so the others can't hear. "She told me all about…umm…their liberal beliefs." *Bigamy? Swinging? God, I hope it doesn't involve the goats.*

His eyes widen. "And?"

"And I'm not quite sure what she meant."

He lets out an embarrassed laugh and sits back into his lounger, pulling me onto his lap and into his arms. "You look terrified. They have other partners, but it's cool. They've always done it."

"And you?" *Please say no. Please say no.*

He holds me tighter. He wraps his hands around my waist, under my T-shirt, keeping me warm. "Oh God no, you don't have to worry about that. One girlfriend at a time is more than enough work for me."

Girlfriend? Is that why he finds it so hard to commit. Has he always been taught there might be someone else, someone better, around the corner?

His sisters beckon us over, as they move on to another classic campfire song, and we leave it there. I've had more than enough relationship talk for one day. And I've almost, maybe, earned the title of 'girlfriend', which is the perfect way to end the day.

Chapter Nine

Day two of our adventures in France is decidedly calmer than day one. We're allowed to get up at a reasonable hour, and the fresh bread Linda made last night is sitting on the table, ready to be spread with homemade cherry jam.

"Do you like it?" she asks, as I finish my last mouthful.

"Delicious, thank you." I raise my hand to my chin as I try my best not to talk with my mouth full.

"We're going to need Sophie today. We've still got so much to do to prepare for the party, and it's all hands on deck," she adds as she whisks my plate away.

"No problem with us," his dad replies. "We'll get far more work done without her." He laughs and winks at me. He's joking, but where's the lie?

The men head off to do their work, something about checking fences. I'm glad not to have gone today. It's even hotter outside than it was yesterday.

G's mom and sisters have emptied out an old barn, and they've been cleaning it for the last few days now. All it needs now is a decorative touch.

"So, you're from LA?" asked G's sister, Monica, as she balances precariously on a wonky ladder.

"Yes, but I've lived there since I was fourteen," I reply, steadying her with one hand and passing up thorny branches with the other. My hands are shredded, but the aesthetic is amazing.

"Oh," she says. "So, your family are Californians too?"

"No, not at all," I reply. "They still live in Illinois. I moved there alone — well, supervised until the age of sixteen by paid guardians, then I was kind of on my own."

"What?" cries Linda, listening to our conversation. She stomps over towards us, her eyes wide in confusion. "You've been on your own since you were fourteen?"

"Pretty much. Both my parents worked full-time, so it's not very easy for them to free up any time to visit me."

"You're not close, then?" she asks, sounding like it is the most incredulous thing she's ever heard.

"I suppose not. They kind of lost interest in me."

Linda doesn't reply. She pulls me in for the biggest bear hug, followed by Monica and Courtney, until we form a giant hug blob with me at the center.

This kind of emotion isn't what I signed up for when I came here. I choke back my tears, swallowing them down with all the other pent-up feelings I have roiling away in my gut. I am starting to become very attached to this family, and that is a dangerous move.

G hasn't been clear on his feelings, beyond the fact that he wants to keep me around for a while. It won't do to start imagining what it would be like to stay in the embrace of this familial cocoon.

I get back to what I am doing. G's sisters have gathered some kind of climbing plant from the farm grounds, and we are wrapping it around the branches, which are wrapped around the barn's wooden beams. It's certainly a lot of work for just a party.

Once the fairy lights are up, though, this place is going to be magical.

The next job is preparing food for over a hundred people. This is Linda's domain, and we're there to follow orders. My job is to peel three pails worth of potatoes to make a salad. It isn't the most complicated job, but it means I can sit and observe G's family as they interact with each other.

His twin sisters' respective characters are wildly different. Monica is a thinker. She asks questions, ponders stuff. Courtney is loud and brash. They are blonde and curvy, like their mother, with long hair and big breasts that are held in by little or no bras under their linen shirts.

Both girls, despite their age, still live at home. That says something about their relationship with their parents. Mine couldn't even wait until I was an adult to get rid of me.

What strikes me is that for the first time in as long as I can remember, I am making friends outside of the industry, and none of these people are under any obligation to be nice to me — at least not as nice as they've been since I got here.

I haven't at any point in the last few days felt as if G's family are making an effort. They genuinely seem to like me. That's something I've never experienced before.

I don't want the day to end. I want to be part of this for as long as they want me. And yet, at the same time, the idea of committing to any kind of relationship, whether it be friendship or otherwise, scares the crap out of me. When your fair-weather friends forget you exist, it doesn't matter, but when you get attached, the eventual separation is much harder to live with. I prefer, in general, not to get attached.

* * * *

August 8, nearly midnight

His whole family have gone bowling tonight to kick off the birthday celebration. I decided to stay behind, alone, feigning a migraine. Going out as a family is such a personal thing to do. Despite their insistence, I'm still very much a stranger to them.

Being alone isn't unusual for me, I lie out under the stars, listening to the eerie sounds of the farm at night, take a picture and post it with the caption, 'A million stars in the sky and you chose mine'. This group of people have chosen to accept me into their homes and their hearts, and I'll never forget that.

I put down my phone and let the cool night air send me to sleep. I am serene. I am safe.

G pecks me lightly on the lips. "Shee, wake up. It's time to go to bed." *Ugh. I don't want to.* The lounger by the pool is the perfect place to sleep in this heat. It's refreshing outside, exactly the right kind of warm. "Come on, sleepyhead. Let's get you upstairs."

I fell asleep under the stars, only to be woken by a kiss from a knight in a Henley shirt. That's the best kind of knight—the whisk-you-up-in-his-arms, Henley-wearing kind.

He carries me, my arms draped around his neck, to our bedroom. "You smell like beer and tacos."

I can feel his smile against my cheek. "It's my signature cologne."

"Mm-m." I snuggle into his neck

"You like that? I can order some in and we can get freaky with the spicy sauce if you like?" he adds. *Oh, we're going to get freaky all right.*

I play with his hair, twirling it around my fingers. "Did you have fun tonight?"

"Not as much fun as I'd have had with you. Are you feeling better?"

"Huh." *What? Oh shit.* Note to self—don't lie to your boyfriend then completely forget. "Oh, yeah, took a tablet and my headache's all gone." He lays me down on the bed and begins to undress me. "You don't have to do that."

"I'm enjoying it." He sinks his hand behind me to unclip my bra and brushes his lips across mine. "I miss you. We've hardly spent any time together since we got here." That isn't entirely true, but we haven't been alone together all day. "I miss touching you."

I like that he needs to be with me. "I know. Me too. Tomorrow is going to be another busy day—or so your mom says—so we can't even sneak off and do naughty stuff in the forest."

He raises his eyebrows. "What kind of naughty stuff?"

I unbutton his trousers and slide my hand into his boxers, wrapping my fingers around his dick. "This."

"That's pretty naughty." He gasps into the last word as I swipe my finger gently around the tip of his cock. "I'm pretty sure I can make time for that in my schedule tomorrow."

He lands his mouth on mine, and we rid ourselves of any leftover clothing. He pulls away, leans back a little, taking in my body.

"You make me feel so beautiful when you do that."

"Ah, you were already beautiful. You didn't need to date me to find that out." He says things like that and it's just... *Oh. My. God. How am I supposed to not fall in love with this man?*

G is a man who takes his time. He doesn't throw me onto the bed and ravage me. He slowly takes in my body, appreciating every inch of it, before getting down to the good stuff. And I don't mind. I don't mind that we're not jumping each other's bones at every opportunity.

There's something about the anticipation of great sex that makes me want to do it less than when I was with crappier lovers.

Weird, I know, but hear me out.

Like, I know it's going to be good, I know I'm going to be spent, physically and emotionally, when we're finished, and it makes me want to savor it more.

When you're desperately hoping for an orgasm, you kind of want to keep doing it, but when you know that multiple mind-blowing orgasms are on the menu, you want to be in top form.

"Talk to me. Tell me how it feels. Tell me when it's too much. Tell me when you want more." His hand is already between my legs, his thumb strumming my clit, barely touching it, brushing past with every stroke. He bites the tip of my nipple, tugging on it, as he enters me with his fingers.

How can I want more when everything he is doing is blowing my mind? "This. I want *this*." The now-familiar feeling of the orgasm rising in me, the blood rushing to my pussy, makes me gasp. I want to come again and again to his touch.

He is never rushed. There's no quick rub of my dry clitoris with a spit-covered finger, then a condom, then sex. He wants this. He wants me to come for him, then, when he knows I'm ready, he'll make love to me, slowly, until I come again.

"Come for me, Sophie," he whispers as my body shakes and trembles in his hands. He lifts his thumb and caresses the orgasm from my core with his fingers.

He turns away to grab a condom. "Let me do it," I say. "I want to."

Sex, as I am learning, is a collaborative affair. G's words echo in my mind from the first time we'd made love.

"It's not about lasting the longest or having the biggest dick. It's about pleasure. Everybody's pleasure."

Neither of those, as it turns out, are an issue.

It hasn't ever occurred to me that even the simple act of putting on the condom could be part of that pleasure. We don't have to rush, and it doesn't have to be a chore. I make damn sure, with the help of my mouth and my hands, that his dick is good and hard before I unroll the condom down to his balls.

I climb right on top of it. He sits up, feathering kisses along the crux of my neck, and I ride him. The pleasures of the moment almost make me forget my aching muscles. *I will pay for this tomorrow.*

All that matters right at this moment is the beautiful feeling of G's cock inside me and the second orgasm coursing through my body as he once again brings me to completion.

My perception of sex has changed entirely. I am not waiting for him to come. I am doing everything in my power to make it happen and to make it as enjoyable for him as I can.

I ride him harder and harder, grinding down onto him with my hips, listening to every pleasured moan and reacting to it until he can't take it anymore. Our ancient French bed creaks and moans along with us, alerting the rest of the house to our business, but I don't care. My sole mission is to give G the best orgasm of his life — and from his muffled cries as he finally releases into me, I've done a fucking good job.

Chapter Ten

August 9, 10 a.m.

This morning is all hands on deck as the final preparations for the party are underway. Friends and family members are due to arrive this afternoon, then a long weekend of eating, drinking and merrymaking will begin.

G and his brother are in charge of putting out tables and chairs in the barn, and the twins and I are in charge of setting up some large tents in the back field.

"Can I ask you a question?" Courtney, the more extroverted of the two sisters, chatters away as we work. She is holding the pins at an angle while I hammer them into the ground.

"You just did," I reply, with a smile. This is going to be one of those 'what's it like to be famous?' questions. I can sense it.

"What's it like, you know, being famous? Are you rich? Do you get free stuff?"

Boom...there it is.

We move to the next tent. "Don't you ask your brother these questions?" *Can you, though, go ask him instead of me? Please.*

She hesitates. "He's not *famous* famous, like you. He's just well-known." *Burn.*

"Well, I don't know what to tell you, really. It's weird that whenever I go out in public, everybody already knows who I am. I've been famous for a long time, so I'm kind of used to it, but sometimes it still takes me by surprise." She nods and waits for me to answer the other questions. "Do you really want to know if I'm rich? I don't think about it that much, which means I probably am. I don't come from money or anything. My parents are just like yours."

"But are you a millionaire?" *Straight in with the literal money-shot.*

"Uh, yes. But I also have to spend money. I have a personal assistant and I have a property in California that has to be looked after when I'm not there. I also pay taxes. It's way more complicated than it sounds." Like *'get yourself a good accountant'* type complicated.

She grimaces. "Oh, I didn't really think of it like that. What about free stuff? I know Gil gets a lot of free clothes and stuff."

"Oh yeah, that's real. My PA and my manager pass things on to me all the time, and if I like them, I stick them on Insta. Otherwise, I send a thank you note and forget about it. I guess that is kind of cool." From the look on her face, it's very cool. "Shall we take a selfie and share it?"

"Can we?" They both jump in beside me and we take a couple of pictures.

"Girls, stop bothering Sophie and get back to work." Linda isn't taking anybody's shit today. "Sophie, I need a hand with something back at the house."

I put down my mallet and follow her out of the field. "Is it cooking related? You know I can't cook."

"No." She stops and gives me a motherly smile — like when you get a bad grade, or your crush turns you down. I've been in enough teen TV shows to know that look. "I'm letting you off early. Our guests should be here soon and that includes Juliette. I thought you might want to freshen up."

"Should I be worried about her?"

She shakes her head. "Oh no, I don't think so. They were together a good couple of years, but it did end amicably, so there might be some residual feelings. I wanted to give you the advantage. I like you, Sophie. I thought you were going to be some big-shot actress from Hollywood, but you're...different. You're good for my Guillaume. He's definitely sexually satisfied, which is half the job when it comes to men."

Uh-huh. Hmm. "Thank you?" Okay, we really needed to work on being a little quieter in the future. And what does she mean by 'give me the advantage'? *Ugh.*

I skulk up to our room. This afternoon calls for a dress. Something a little sexy, but pretty enough to not look like I am trying too hard.

Who am I kidding? I need to look drop-dead gorgeous — which isn't easy when you've got pig poop under your nails and sunburned everything. *I need a plan of action.*

Chapter Eleven

August 9, 2 p.m.

There's no handbook for meeting your boyfriend's ex-girlfriend, nor for boyfriends themselves. You just work it out as you go along, and, frankly, the idea of it exhausts me.

I waft down the stairs in a pretty cotton summer dress, just as the guests begin to arrive. From the look on G's face, I've chosen well. It's a little bit transparent with the sun behind me and perfectly pretty but with a décolleté that shows off my best—and most expensive—assets. He glances up at me as I come down the stairs and does a double take. *Mission accomplished.*

"We need to get outside to greet everybody. People have already started arriving." He slips an arm around my back and snuggles his nose into my neck, inhaling my very expensive perfume and letting out just the tiniest moan. "God, you're...mm-m." The grip on my back tightens. Have I gone too far? I don't want to attract too much attention to myself, either. There are going to be a lot of people around this weekend, and I'd only wanted to remind G what he has, not entice others to join the fray.

A minibus arrives and a group of tired-looking, sweaty French people pile out. A beautiful woman, probably about our age, steps out of the side door, and G's hand drops from my back.

Juliette.

She is very French — tanned skin, long dark hair that looked like it's been spun from silk and a figure that brings the whole thing together. Perfection. "Guillaume!" she cries, raising her hands in the air, ready for a hug. He runs forward into her embrace, and I suddenly cease to exist.

Four or five more cars draw up into the car park, and within minutes, the place is awash with excitable French people kissing each other and tired-looking Americans, fresh off the plane, looking for somewhere to put their baggage.

And I am in the middle of it, looking and smelling like a dream — like the best bit of bait, hanging off the hook, floating in the river, completely and utterly unprotected from what is to follow.

Hugs. Unwanted, invasive hugs. And, because this is France, kisses too.

Anxiety rises within me. My body stiffens, my breathing becomes irregular, my heart makes an attempt at a getaway via my chest. I rub my palms together. *This is fine. It's fine. It's only G's family and friends.* I look around for Monica or Courtney or any member of G's family to hide behind, but they're all busy helping people with luggage or catching up with old friends.

I can't even see G now. There must be at least fifty people milling around the place, loudly catching up on each other's news. He's lost in the crowd.

"You are Sophie Smith?" asks a young girl with a strong French accent, probably no older than ten or eleven.

"Yes." I smile for her, as is required.

She holds up her phone and says, "Can I?"

"Sure." The first selfie of the day, and she is perfectly sweet.

Then come the rest. A group of five or so guys, American, come barreling toward me.

"You're Polly, right, from that show?" Without wondering as to whether he should, or even proffering a 'please' or 'thank you', this guy sticks his arm around my shoulder, pulls me into his chest and takes a selfie. And so, it begins.

I am passed from arm to arm, not a single consideration for whether I want to or not. Grab, chest hold, photo and so on and so on. Intrigued by what's happening, other guests follow suit and assume that, as I've given permission to everybody else, that they too can pull me in closer. The smile on my mouth freezes, and I accept my fate.

So pleased are they to get a photo, and so blinded by my perfect smile, courtesy of extensive dental work six years ago, that they don't even notice the tears silently rolling down my face.

It isn't the fans. Shit happens when you're famous, and you get used to it. It's that G didn't even stay by my side. He hasn't once come back to check on me.

I am alone.

Eventually the crowd subsides as they haul their baggage to their tents, and the car park clears. I stand there, disheveled, waiting for G to come back to me, but he's no longer there.

I lift my skirt a little, walk down the lane and along the path to the woods. My pretty heels dig into the ground where pools have formed from a late-night storm. The warm mud sticks to my shoes and ankles and encourages the dust from the rest of the path to climb up my shins.

I find our favorite clearing and lie under the sun, feeling it burn my face, listening to nothing but the chirping of crickets and the distant sound of the donkeys from the farm making that 'hee-haw' sound, disturbed by the presence of so many people in the field next to theirs.

I close my eyes. The warm summer breeze blows across me, calming my heart. I want to stay here forever, untouched, alone, never to be disturbed again. Like Sleeping Beauty, thorny bushes will grow around me, and only my true love can break through and free me. I want the damp grass to suck up all the fingerprints from my shoulders and wipe off the smell of unwanted body odors from my cheeks.

At some point someone will notice that I'm not there, my phone will beep and I will have to go back. But for now, I lie there, silent and unmoving, soaking up the freedom of total solitude, breathing long deep breaths of pure French air and letting the tears run down my cheeks and into the ground below.

* * * *

August 9, 4 p.m.

In the end, the warm summer sun is what makes me traipse back to the house. There's only so long that I can stay outside before I turn into even more of a lobster, and even in my present mood, I have to accept defeat.

Everybody is in the garden, helping themselves to the first of several buffets that will be presented this weekend. The wine is flowing, the guitars are out and the party has definitely begun.

G and his brother are in the pool with the American guys from earlier, diving and jumping on each other's backs, splashing anybody who dares to approach them.

I serve myself a glass of water and go to sit by the pool, pulling off my heels and wiping the dust from my ankles.

"You are Sophie? The girlfriend of Guillaume."

I look up. "Yes."

"I am Juliette." I know it's her accent, but it comes out as if she is regal in some way — as if she is addressing her subjects.

The politest of my fake smiles forms on my lips. "I know."

She throws a smile right back and scoots down onto the lounger next to me. "You are very beautiful."

"Thank you, so are you."

Too beautiful, like way too beautiful. Like, if you can tone it down a little, that would be great.

She looks over at the boys, who haven't even acknowledged our presence. "Guillaume, he is" — she hesitates, searching for the word — "difficult."

Is that the word she meant to use?

"Difficult?"

She scrunches up her nose, takes a deep breath and pauses before continuing. "He wants to be like his family, he wants to *honneur* their ideas about love and *liberté*, but he is a *chou*."

"A shoe?" I point to my foot.

"No, no." She lets out a coy giggle. "A *chou*, like a vegetable."

I nod. "Uh-huh." I still have no idea what she means.

"He loves deep. And *dur*...hard. Too hard, too much."

"Maybe for you." I shake my head. "Not so much me." She pulls her legs up in front of her and winds her arms around her knees, shaking her head as she does so.

"Oh, no, no. You see? He loves me so much he *couché*..." She hesitates again.

Voulez-vous coucher avec moi? One of the few well-known French phrases in my repertoire. "Slept?"

"Yes. He slept with my best friend."

What? How is that 'loving her too much'? "Wow. Okay." Now I'm intrigued. "Go on. I'm listening."

She laughs and shakes her hands as if to wipe away what she's said and start again. "I say it all wrong. Guillaume, he is beautiful and sweet, but he has no *reference*. He thinks he must be free, like the birds, but he cannot understand his heart, so when his heart is full, he *paniques* and he runs away."

"Oh!" *Oooooh. Okay. Right. Got you.*

"So, I want to say, because he is flirting with me and I say, no, Guillaume, don't do that." She points her finger at me, demonstrating how she chastised him. "I want to say that it stops here. We are girl power. Nobody sleeps with Guillaume."

"Except me."

She holds her arms out wide, waiting to see if a hug is in order. "Excepting you." For the first time that day I have a proper, welcome hug from a friend.

I've met Juliette...and it is awesome.

And devastating at the very same time.

Chapter Twelve

Shortly after my conversation with Juliette, G emerges from the pool, dripping wet and looking like that fantasy that pops into my mind. You remember, the slow-motion one.

I'm so angry with him but I also kind of want to bang him.

It's not easy being me.

He walks up to us like nothing's happened since he'd abandoned me in a car park—leaving me to fend off his touchy-feely friends alone—while he flirted, and would probably have done more if she'd so desired, with his ex.

"Shee. Juliette. Cool." He doesn't look like he thinks it's cool. He looks like he wants to run away and hide but is playing it by ear, seeing if we've talked before taking for the hills.

Too late, G. You're busted.

"Gil," I reply, with a smile. He flinches. Pretty sure, in the many months since we met, I've never referred to him by that name. "You two have probably got so much catching up to do. I'll leave you to it." I stand up and link my arm through one of his friend's arms. "Now who out of you lot is going to get me a drink. I hear there are shots in the second barn down."

We amble off toward the open bar, leaving G to gape like a fish out of water.

"Wait!" shouts Juliette. "What are shots? I want shots!" she cries, racing after us. She runs up beside me, links her arm through mine and joins the party. I glanced back at G.

Who's alone now?

The barn with the bar is darker and cooler than outside. It has a bit of a club vibe going on. A local rock group is playing seventies hits. People are dancing and drinking. Linda is making out in the corner of the room with a man who is absolutely *not* G's dad. And by making out, I mean visible tongues are involved.

I'm not close to my parents and I one hundred percent wouldn't be surprised if they cheated, but I could not get on board with having to see it. I'm not saying that it's why G is so fucked up in the relationship department, but I'm quite sure my therapist would have a few thoughts on the matter.

G finally catches up with us. He grabs a shot off the bar and downs it, then another. "Can we talk?" He glances over my shoulder at his mother, rolls his eyes and picks up a couple of glasses of champagne. "Outside?"

"Sure." We leave Juliette purring into the ears of her new-found admirers and go back out under the blazing sun. "We need to find the shade. I can't cope with this heat."

A storage barn, a few hundred yards down, does the trick.

"Did I do something wrong?" asks G.

Still trying to figure out what I know, huh?

"You're kidding, right?" The audacity. "You abandoned me in the car park for your ex-girlfriend, who, I have since discovered, you then proceeded to flirt with and more, suggesting, if I understand her broken English correctly, something involving her tent and your naked asses."

He shakes his head. "I never said... I mean, she probably... She must have misunderstood." The guy is sweating.

"Did she misunderstand when you told her you loved her, then slept with her best friend?" I lean back onto a rusty old tractor. "She must be pretty dumb, not understanding a word you say and thinking you're a serial cheater."

"Fuck, fuck, fuck." He throws his hands in the air and loses his balance. His champagne glass crashes to the floor. He leans against the cold, stone walls to get his balance, kicking at the glass to form a pile. "I'm sorry. I'm *so* sorry. I don't know what I was thinking. I haven't seen her since we split up, and I was thrown for a minute. I guess I got carried away. I didn't mean it, and I wouldn't have done it. I know you don't believe me, but what I had with her and what I have with you aren't the same at all." He goes to grab my shoulder, but I pull away.

"No."

I should be grateful, perhaps, that he isn't trying to make excuses.

"I get really close to someone, then I get scared and do really stupid shit. That's why I kept telling you I couldn't commit, and that's why I kept insisting we're friends. But we aren't, and I almost blew it. I fucked up, Shee."

"Oh, you fucked up, big time." He's always been honest in that respect, not committing to us, but there was always a hint of a hope, a comment here and there. *I don't deserve this, though. I deserve some fidelity, don't I?*

He starts to cry, like proper weeping. He's standing there in front of me, all helpless and lost, and I am at a loss for what to do. I want to comfort him, but, shit, I'm still so mad.

"Why, though? Why bring me here? Was it just for sex? Was that all you wanted from me?" I've been a fucking idiot…literally. Drawn in by a cute body and multiple orgasms.

"No, God no. I brought you here because" — he hesitates — "because I can't imagine being without you. When the movie was over, all I could think about was that I wouldn't get to see you every day and it broke me. I need you."

What? I rub my hand across my forehead. My head hurts. "I'm so special and you can't live without me, and yet in ten seconds flat you're trying to fuck someone else." *Does he even hear himself?*

He tries once again to touch me, reassure me, but I push him back, splashing champagne everywhere.

"It's like my brain does this thing. Like, the minute I fall in love, *bam*, I've got to ruin it." He wipes the tears from his face and takes a breath. "I'm so sorry, Shee. I wouldn't have done it. I promise."

"She turned you down and you got busted. That's why you're sorry." I start to walk away.

He comes after me and grabs my hand. "Don't go. Please. I'm begging you. Let me prove it to you. Let me prove that I can be who you need."

"Well, you already failed at that today. Get out your phone."

He wipes his face with the back of his hand, sniffs. "What?"

I soften my tone. He might be a fucked-up asshole, but he is *my* fucked-up asshole. He looks so broken. Despite my anger, my heart is hurting for him. "Just get out your phone and check your Insta. I want to show you something."

"Why?" He frowns, pulls out his phone from his back pocket, swipes it. "What am I looking for?"

"You're looking for selfies with me and those friends of yours back there."

He scrolls down the photos of his friends, not getting it at first, then he spots all the unwanted hugs.

"Oh, shit." He closes his eyes and hangs his head in shame. "I'm sorry, Shee. In their defense, I don't think they meant any harm." I wait for him to elaborate on this pitiful excuse. "No. I know. I mean, you're right. They shouldn't have touched you without your permission. I get it. I'll talk to them."

His hand is still holding on to mine, our fingers barely touching. I am still pulling away.

"You're not my bodyguard. I don't expect you to protect me from the fans. And I don't expect them to know that I don't like to be touched that way. It's…" I paused. I'm cracking. I needed to cry too, and it's choking my words. The two of us will be blubbering messes by the end of this conversation. "It's my life. It's been like that since forever. But here. Here, where you told me I would be safe. Here, where you *promised* me I didn't have to worry about things like that. I didn't think I would have to be *her*."

"Shee." He drops my hand, holds out his arms, and I take a step forward. I so desperately want this moment to be over and forgotten and to go back to how we were this morning, lying in each other's arms, with not a care in the world.

"I thought I could just be me."

Saying it is like a release. Admitting that I don't want to be the selfie-taking, always smiling perfect Sophie Smith is like taking a lifelong back-breaking weight off my shoulders. I hate her. I hate Sophie Smith, the actress, influencer and all-around eternally happy being.

My sobs are loud and hard, only punctuated by G's apologies ringing in my ears as he takes me into his arms and holds my shaking body.

We're both total and utter train wrecks. The player who doesn't want to play and the celebrity who wants to be left alone.

There's a strange comfort in finding somebody who is as fucked up as I am. Misery loves company.

"You want to go get another drink?" he asks, wiping the tears from my face as we come down from our sobfest. "Or something to eat?" I'm still sheltered in the cocoon of his arms. It's warm and welcoming and safe.

Safe as it can be when I know that our relationship is held together by the thinnest thread.

I shake my head. "I think I want to be alone for a while. Is that okay?"

"Sure. If that's what you want. I'm sorry, Shee. I swear, it was a momentary lapse of judgment. All of it. It won't happen again."

"Promise you won't seduce anybody while I'm gone?" I crack a smile, and he reciprocates. He leans down and places a kiss on my tear-filled face.

Fucked up, we truly are.

"Harsh, but fair." He lets go of me, jumps up onto the tractor and places his hand on his heart. "I faithfully promise not to seduce anybody but Shee-who-must-be-obeyed — forever and always."

The tractor makes a cracking noise as it strains under his weight. "Get down before your hurt yourself."

"Shh, I'm declaring my love."

Love? Please. The guy doesn't know the meaning of the word.

I grab his hand and pull at it. "Stop messing around."

He smiles the kind of smile that makes me forget for an instant that I'm still mad at him and makes me want to kiss that stupid face instead. "Do you love me, too? Shee-Shee?" *He isn't going to get down until I say it, is he?*

"Sure. Now get down off the tractor and go find your friends."

He jumps down. "She loves me, and all is forgiven."

"Don't push your luck," I reply, placing a hand on his back as we walk out of the barn.

He turns around, walking backward and kisses me on the nose. "She loves me," he whispers and runs off back to the bar.

Chapter Thirteen

August 9, 6 p.m.

After all the emotion of the showdown with G, I need to clear my head. I wander around the farm. They've put up barriers so nobody will get the bright idea to go ride the new camel at midnight. I climb over them, still in my bare feet, and head for the llama enclosure. My favorite bunch of wild fluffy beasts are all overjoyed to see me, and they come running up, expecting carrots and hugs.

"No carrots this time, guys," I say, but they stay for the hugs because my ear scritches are unbeaten in this part of France. I sense a pair of eyes watching me from above and look over at my nemesis. He plays it cool, looks away as soon as I turn my head, but I know that he's thinking that he might want to get in on some of those snuggles.

With time on my hands and no desire to go back to the party yet, I sit on a bench next to Tornado's enclosure, lift my feet, wrap my arms around my knees and wait for the day to pass.

I smell his breath before I feel the warm air on my neck. He is standing right behind me, his nose stuck firmly in my hair, having a good sniff.

"Hey, you," I say. "You want a cuddle too?" I lift my hand and place it on my shoulder, not turning my head to look, and he sticks his nose under it. Leaving it there for a good minute or so, we sit and appreciate being two solitary creatures on a French mountain on a summer's evening. After a while, he nuzzles me again, and I turn and scratch the bit behind his ears where he can't reach. He sinks and turns his head to make sure I don't miss any bits.

It's probably been years since this guy has approached a human, and he isn't going to miss out on this opportunity to get as many itches scratched as he can.

"You really do like the ladies, don't you, Romeo." He lets out a snort in reply. "I'll let G know he's got a bit of competition. That might jolt some sense into him. What do you think?"

He snorts again.

"Yeah, I don't think it'll work either, but we have to hope he'll come around. You did." I give my friend a final hug and head back toward the party.

It's time to put my public face back on again.

The afternoon is coming to an end, and after several hours of eating and drinking, the guests are calming down. Some people have gone back to their tents to rest or are using the temporary showers we've installed to clean up and get ready for the evening's festivities.

The party is to last until Sunday afternoon, and it's only Friday. Tonight is pizzas and karaoke, and tomorrow is a quiet day. The guests are either going to sleep or go for walks or help out on the farm. This evening is the big event, where another fifty or so people will arrive. Then Sunday morning is the big clean up, followed by a big goodbye barbecue and life will go back to normal for the Carter family.

I find my shoes by the pool and head upstairs to take a shower of my own. G is asleep in our bed. Naked and, thankfully, alone. From the sound of snoring, the shots and champagne continued after my absence.

I take a long shower. The house is full and the water system entirely unreliable. I don't know when I might get access to hot water again. Then I slip under the sheets next to him.

"Shee?" he murmurs, slipping his arm around my waist.

I don't want him to think that I am not still totally mad at him. "Who were you expecting?"

"You smell beautiful." His words are kind of slurred, either from napping or alcohol — or probably a combination of both.

"You smell like tequila." He smells like warmth and comfort, but I am not going to give him the satisfaction of knowing that.

"Mm-hmm." He snuggles up real close behind me, his excitement at my presence digging into the base of my spine. "I'm sorry I'm such a dumbass. I love you."

"You shouldn't say that unless you mean it." He lays a trail with his tongue from my shoulder to my neck and makes me shake with anticipation.

"I do, though. I've loved you since that first kiss in your trailer. Only I wasn't supposed to love you because that kiss wasn't supposed to mean anything." He slides his dick in between my thighs so it is rubbing against my pussy and drops his hand down to my clit. "I want to…uh… I get it if you don't want to."

My body is already stirring to his touch, my senses heightened. It seems silly to stop now when an orgasm will be imminent.

"This doesn't mean we're good, and it doesn't mean I love you."

"I know." He slides back, rolls away. *Shit. Have I fucked it up?* The now-familiar sound of the condom wrapper ripping says that, no, everything's good.

Sliding back into place, his hand brushes my thigh and settles back down onto my core. Caressing my clit with his fingers, he places the tip of his cock just at my entry and no farther.

Fuck me. My body is screaming for him to enter me, but he doesn't move his hips, building the excitement. He brushes the back of my neck with his lips, sending chills down my spine. I am so ready for him, and yet still he doesn't move.

Just do it. My arousal is peaking. Every nerve in my pussy is charged. He places his other hand on my stomach and fills me, entering me as far as he can. My core tightens and the waves of my orgasm make me shudder and jerk in his arms.

I let out a groan, like my lungs have emptied, throw my head back onto his shoulder as he pumps, again and again into me, letting out his own cries of pleasure.

It is hard and fast, the roughest he has ever been with me. And yet at the same time the utter sensuality of his body, glued to mine, his arms wrapped around me, only the slightest of movements as he plunges into me over and over is so subtle, gentle, tender.

His hand is no longer on my clit but I can feel myself coming again, hard, fast and out of my control.

"Oh my God!" It's powerful and draining, almost painful in its intensity.

I tighten so hard on him that he gasps, like he's searching for air, "Shit. Fuck." He empties into me, still pounding hard. Every single inch of tension in his body releases as he collapses down onto the bed. "You kill me. Fuck."

I roll over. He throws his hand to his forehead and wipes the sweat from his brow.

"Good. It's a reminder of what you'll be missing if you ever even look at another woman."

"It was never just about sex. You know that, right? It was about you. I fell in love with you, long before I got to touch your body, at least, in a sexual way."

I hear my own words echo in my mind.

He lifts his head and plants his mouth onto mine with such passion that it's as if he's using the very last of his energy to accomplish this task.

We kiss for what seems like an eternity, stopping and starting and giggling as we go. Neither of us can stop.

"I need to breathe," I say into his mouth.

"Me too. And I need a shower and another drink."

"I'm pretty sure you don't need another drink," I reply, laughing. "I need one, though."

We shower, again, my third of the day, change into comfy evening clothes and head down to see who's around.

Whether it's guilt, love, lust or all of the above, he can't keep his hands off me. G's love language is touch. There's no doubt about it.

Mine is words of affirmation, just in case you were wondering, but you weren't because it's that obvious, really, isn't it?

He constantly needs to hold me in some way, playing with my fingers if we're sitting next to each other, pulling me onto his lap or the famous palm in the center of my back as we walk into a room.

Right now, his hands are magnetically drawn to every part of my body, and I have the feeling that it's going to be like that all night. *Is it to reassure me that he loves me, or to reassure himself that he's forgiven?*

All I know is that he's the only person in the world who I've ever allowed to touch me in that way, to invade my bubble, and I truly hope he knows it.

Karaoke is a wild affair. It's in the barn bar. Chairs and tables are brought in from outside and a hundred pizzas, delivered by a local restaurant, are cut and ready to be eaten. Pizza flavors here are odd. One of them has a cheesy potato topping—a local specialty—with thick chunks of sausage thrown on top. Beef is popular here too, chunky slices of steak mixed in with melted cheese. There's no way my hips are going to come out of this evening without a few extra inches on them.

Fuck it. It isn't like I'm planning to go back to acting anyway.

I tell G and his friends, one of whom is firmly attached to Juliette by the lips, about my newfound friendship with Tornado. We promise to give the guys a tour of the mini-zoo the next day, on the agreement that they help out with chores. Might as well get some use out of them, seeing as they're drinking their way through the free beer.

G's parents seem to have found each other and are back to looking like they're just a normal married couple, if such a thing exists. Her boyfriend is at a separate table with friends, and I scan the room trying to work out who G's dad is dating.

The whole situation is a mystery to me. How does it work, even? Do they have a night where they can go see their partner? Or do they just pop in when they fancy it? Do they get on or are there jealousies between partner and spouse? So many questions.

A form is passed around and we have to sign up to sing. I try to pass it on and not sign up, but everybody is doing it and they all insist. I'm embarrassed to say that I'm a great singer. In that I'm pretty, I can act and I can sing too.

Sorry.

Now you can see why my sister hates me. I'd hate me if I was my sister, too.

I know some people don't like that kind of thing, especially when you're the only 'celebrity'. It reeks of showing off.

I choose *Everytime* by Britney. It's a mood...mine.

There are some great singers and some terrible ones. The American lads, accompanied by a very out of tune, slightly drunk G and Thibault, sing something from The Blues Brothers and everyone is up and dancing with them.

When my name is called out, there's a hush, as if they're all waiting for the star act. It's horrible, and I hate it. I want to run right out of the room instead of performing for them. Reminding myself that this is me joining in and being part of a family doesn't help.

People will film it.

And people will most certainly tell their friends they went to karaoke and saw Sophie Smith sing.

Then it will, without a doubt, be on Twitter within the hour.

So, it has to be not shit, and that sucks. The temptation to sing badly and do a weird dance is overwhelming, but my grandma's steely-eyed stare glowers down from heaven at me, and so I put on a show.

I sing. They watch in silence. Some people cry. Okay, G cried...like a lot. In his defense, he is absolutely hammered. Then he tells me he loves me again and pulls me onto his lap.

It hasn't been as bad as I thought it would be, and I'm quickly replaced in everybody's hearts by a group of French people singing songs that involved waving napkins in the air and jumping up and down like sardines in a tin.

The karaoke kind of degenerates after that into a mixture of bawdy French and English songs that would make a sailor blush. Most of the time, half the room has no idea what the other half of the room is singing, but they belt out the chorus anyway.

It is one a.m. before everybody starts packing up. G is in charge of helping certain members of his family back to their tents without them falling in ditches or spraining an ankle. To be entirely honest, I'm not sure he's much help to anybody after the number of shots he's ingested tonight, but best of luck to them. I stay behind to help his mom clear up the glasses. They've invested in glassware and plates for the weekend, in an effort to save the planet, but the amount of rinsing and drying that's required will keep her up all night.

"How did it go with Juliette?" she asks, raising her eyebrows in that way that people do when they already know the answer to their question.

"Oh, she's great. I love her. But that's not what you're asking, is it? You knew he'd do something, didn't you?"

"Yes." She puts down her soapy sponge for a second, placing both hands on the sink and taking a deep breath. "When we lived at home, in the US, we kept our personal life secret. Our kids knew that Mom and Dad had boyfriends and girlfriends, but that was it. When we moved here, there was such a sense of freedom. We aren't putting it out there for all to see — the French can be very prudish, you know — but we're far more open about it with our friends. As Guillaume came over with us, he had a more open view of how we live than his brother and sisters."

"But?"

"But he also saw how happy we are compared to how miserable we'd been in the US. He has formed this idea in his mind, which isn't all down to just our love lives. We've got our own business here, a beautiful home in the mountains, all the wine we can drink. He got it into his head that being settled down makes you unhappy and, I think, even though he's chosen a monogamous lifestyle, he can't quite get over the idea that the minute you fall in love, it's all going to go to shit."

Wow. "Okay. So that's why he cheated on Juliette."

She nods. "Maybe. I don't know. He did it in a way that meant they were never getting back together — to make damn sure she didn't want him anymore."

How sad. I know they didn't mean to do it, but his parents had fucked him up good and proper. "And that's why he did what he did today?"

She tilts her head. "So, something did happen?"

"Yeah, but Juliette told him he could" —I bite my tongue—"stuff it. She's one of the good ones."

She smiled. "That she is."

We carry on doing the dishes for a good hour and chatting about life, love and everything. Linda is exactly the kind of person who I would have adored to have as my mom. She's so easy to talk to and so smart. Plus, she has *so much* love to give. Admittedly, she's sharing it far and wide, but she has two partners, as well as a doting husband, who are as kind and sweet as her, so why not?

In the end, once everything is done, the sun is peeking up and neither of us has slept. "Go to bed for a few hours. A quiet day, just chores and final preparations for tomorrow night."

"Are you going to bed?" If I know this woman, she'll not sleep until Monday, and even then, she'll be up at five a.m. the next day.

"Just a couple of hours, then I've got to make breakfast for fifty."

I pretend to bow down to her. "You're like a machine. Where do you get the energy?"

"It's not always like this. I'm normally in bed nice and early, whoever that's with." She winks at me and nudges my elbow as we walk out of the barn into the dewy morning and breathe in the cold, fresh air.

I put my hand to my mouth in pretend shock and giggle at her joke. "Thank you, Linda, for being so good to me, taking me in and, well, you know, looking after me."

"I think my boy's in love with you, and I can see why. You're special, Sophie." It's the first time in my life somebody has uttered those words that I don't want to scream in their face. "And I think you need a mom in your life too, if I'm not wrong. I'd be happy to be that person. I've got lots of space in my heart for everyone."

I hug her, which takes her by surprise. I feel her chuckle as I wrap my arms tightly around her.

Another thing that I would never normally do. I am fully initiated into the cult of Linda.

"I do. Thank you. I really do."

Chapter Fourteen

August 10, 9 a.m.

After finally getting some sleep and waking up with a cotton mouth and a horny boyfriend, I have a freezing cold shower—no surprise there with all the guests in the house—and head out with my list of chores. It hasn't even taken a week for me to become part of this family. *Wild. Just wild.*

My new best friend has never allowed anybody to stay longer than five minutes in his enclosure, so Linda and Bob have signed me up for an afternoon of bad-tempered llama brushing—he's getting the makeover, not me—then getting as much weeding in his enclosure as he will let me do without him getting grumpy again and throwing me out.

Turns out that once llamas have fallen in love with you, they won't leave you alone for a second. Tornado does not like the hat on my head protecting me from the hot sun and takes to grabbing it off my head, ripping out half of my hair with it and tossing it to the goats. Then he nibbles my shoulders until I give him carrots.

Of all the pictures of me that have been taken this weekend and put online, the ones that will probably be most remembered by the public are of me being assaulted by a lovesick llama, then chasing him around a field, trying to get my hat back.

Once I've gotten well and truly grubby, I need to have another shower and get ready for the evening's festivities. The party is being held in the big barn. All the tables and chairs have been moved back in there, and a party planner, hired from the nearest big town, has decorated them beautifully. The plants that Linda, the girls and I hung from the rafters, sprinkled with fairy lights, has turned it into the most beautiful rustic ballroom.

Tonight is formal wear. I pack G's tux up and send him off to drink beers and get ready with the boys. Juliette and the twins join me for champagne and gossip.

"So, how's it going with your new man?" I ask.

Juliette, painting Courtney's toenails, looks up and smiles coyly. "He is not my man. He is just a summer love. You say 'a squish' — no, 'a crush'."

Monica and Courtney both have dates coming tonight, so they have to look perfectly beautiful, which isn't difficult. Taking after their American mother, they look so vastly different from the French women I've met since I arrived. They stand out, in a good way. Their hair is perfectly twirled, thanks to my very expensive straightener, and make-up perfectly done, thanks to Juliette. They both looked stunning.

We're four strong, beautiful women and we know it. We're going to own this party.

"What are you guys wearing? I brought two dresses, and I can't decide." I open my wardrobe and get them out. One is a sleek, dark green number that I wore to an award's ceremony a couple of years back. It gives great boobs but is a bit long. The other is still fancy but knee length and a little more like a party dress. It was sent to me for a gala dinner, but I've never worn it. "Red or green?"

"Oh my God, those dresses are stunning," says Monica, sitting up and reaching out to touch the fabric.

"Right?" adds Courtney. "Either one will look amazing on you."

I get out my heels and hold them up to the dresses. The green is definitely doing it for me. "Which one do you think G will like most?" The girls all made fake vomiting motions with their hands and mouths. "I get it. I'm stupid and in love. I want to look nice for him."

They all side-eye each other. I know what they're thinking — that I am setting myself up for a fall. But it isn't true. G is working on his issues, or so he repeatedly tells me. This time I will tame the wild animal that is Guillaume Carter and put a stop to his cycle of commitment-phobic cheating.

If I say it enough times it'll come true, right? How many women have said that in their lives? This time it's different. *Fuck. I'm a cliché.*

We get tipsy on champagne and make ourselves more beautiful than is truly necessary, then we head down to the barn. The party is starting with cocktails at eight, a full four-course meal at nine-thirty, followed by dancing late into the night.

* * * *

People are already filling the car park, as more guests arrive and there's a hint of excitement in the air. The four of us stride into the barn looking like Charlie's Angels but with way more sass. The boys at the bar turn to look and several jaws drop to the floor. We don't let them know, but the sight of all those tight muscly bodies squeezed into tuxes is pretty jaw-dropping too. Monica and Courtney are set up with two brothers from a neighboring farm and, my God, they scrub up well.

I spot G, at the back of the group, and when he looks up from his drink? Well, let's just say that he clearly isn't disappointed.

"It's going to be a shame to have to take you back up to our room and rip that dress off of you, but I'm obligated to inform you that that's what I'm going to do."

"You'll do no such thing. It took me half an hour to squeeze my body into the built-in corset in this dress because of all the food your mom has fed me since we got here."

"You are kind of bursting out of it." His glance sinks down to my ample breasts. "In a good way."

He slides his hand around the base of my spine, giving my butt a teasing squeeze and hands me a glass of champagne. "You look pretty gorgeous yourself," I whisper into his ear. He smiles, puts down his drink and runs a hand through his dark curls. *Holy fuck.* "You can keep the bowtie on tonight, make it classy."

He chuckles and pecks me on the cheek. "I love you, Shee."

My stomach does a roll.

I don't know why, but this time is the one for me.

The one that counts.

It feels right, as if I'd been waiting for permission to truly accept what he has to offer, and now my mind is open to it.

Everyone steps in around us and leans in for a picture, smiling and waving as Linda, looking stunning herself, takes a group photo.

"I love you, too, G, and I mean it this time," I reply.

I'm going to need a copy of that photo. The look on his face is priceless.

We stand around chatting while we wait to be seated. I've put my phone in my clutch bag, which is hanging from my wrist. It hasn't stopped beeping since I'd arrived, so I take a moment to see what the hell is going on.

I must have a thousand notifications and a least a dozen messages from my manager, Suzy.

They're canceling the show, the one that made me a household name around the world. And, what is *more* urgent, as she recounts in the eleventy million messages she's left, is that they want me and 'Marcus', my first ever on-screen other half, back for the final few episodes. He's up for it. Rehearsals start Monday. The script is being sent by courier.

I stare down at my phone then up at my new friends and at G. He'll be heading to North America in October for some project he's signed up for, but we have plans for the next couple of months. We are going to visit the rest of Europe, maybe rent a house somewhere on the shoreline of a Norwegian fjord, and just enjoy the tranquility of life, books and freedom.

We have it all planned.

The sense of dread envelops me as if I'm back under the freezing cold shower from this afternoon, turning my blood cold and making my legs give way.

Sensing my distress, G looks over and smiles, in a 'you okay?' way. I shove my phone into my bag and walk over to the group. This is not going to ruin such a beautiful night. Telling her 'no' can wait until tomorrow.

The food is divine, and the company is perfect. G's hand is constantly on my knee, entwined with my fingers or over my shoulder — and it fills my heart. There's a comfort in knowing you're loved, especially when they ask nothing of you in return.

Grandma was the only person who had loved me growing up, and even then, it had been conditional to the point of exhaustion. That's no way to show you care.

We drink and we eat and we dance. We sneak off and make love against the rusty old tractor in the storage barn. Then we dance some more. At the end of the evening, we sit on loungers around the fire pit and share stories with his friends. It is an immensely beautiful moment in my life and something that could not have prepared me for what comes next.

"You should go."

"What?" As we've found ourselves alone under the starlit night, our friends having gone off to do their own thing, I've finally told G about all the messages.

He looks me right in the eyes. "You should go. You should do the show. Can you imagine how amazing it would be to have Polly and Marcus on screen together again? The fans will go wild."

"I told you that I'm giving up acting. Once the hiatus is over, we'll do the promotion for the movie, then I'm walking away." I can't do it. I can't be *her* any longer.

He understands that, right? He understands my desperate need to move on from this life that I never wanted and to become someone I can love.

He frowns. "I have to go back in a couple of months anyway. It won't be long until we see each other again, if that's what you're worried about." *Oh. Right. It's all about him.*

I sit up and push his hands off me. "That's not the point. What about traveling? What about my perfect hiatus? What about me not being Sophie Smith, Actress, Celebrity, Influencer?" Has he not listened to a single fucking word I've said since we'd gotten here? *For fuck's sake.*

"Okay, the traveling I get." He shakes his head at me, raising his voice a little. "But giving up your job, when your career is on a high? That's just *wrong*. You're living the dream, Sophie. There's a million other women out there who'd sell their right arm to have what you have, and you just want to give it up and walk away."

Wrong. *Wrong?*

It's not the dream, though. It never was. It's somebody else's dream, not mine. I can't do this anymore.

He doesn't see me at all. I get up and stand over him. "You don't love me."

He puts out his hands, trying to pull me back onto him. "Shee, wait. Let's talk about this."

"Is this because of what I said earlier, because I told you I love you? Is that why you want me to go?" Have I been foolish enough to believe that he wouldn't run for the hills as soon as I uttered those three special words?

He shook his head. "No. No, Shee, not at all. I just don't get why you want to give it all up. Think about how much we could achieve *together*."

"I was... I was planning so many amazing things, and you were in every one of them. I would have been happy to stand by and let you hit the heights of fame, get the best roles, be the best actor you can be, and I would have supported you through every moment of it. I would have followed you anywhere in the world. But that's because I love you, I listen to you and I want what's best for you. You want none of that for me." My heart is hurting. It is breaking in two, and he can't even see it — or simply doesn't care. All he can think about is how it's going to affect *him*.

I storm off without a backward glance. *Fuck him. Fuck him for every lie he's spun me.*

The caterers are packing up the last of their stuff in the car park. I ask, in my terrible French, if I can hitch a lift to wherever they're going. "Runes," says the driver, looking as though he is mightily puzzled as to why anybody would want to go there.

"Can you take me to Runes?" Anywhere has to be better than here.

"Okay." He shrugs, in the most Gallic way possible, and we drive off into the night. My mind goes back to the girls and how they'd mocked my confidence in mine and G's relationship.

I've been such a fool.

Chapter Fifteen

August 11, 5 a.m.

I'm normally pretty careful about safety but getting into a van with a stranger and going to a village in the middle of nowhere after a night of drinking has to be pretty high on the list of stupidest things I'd ever done.

Runes, as it turns out, is even more desolate than G's village. The caterer nudges me awake when we arrive and asks me something I don't understand.

I smile and scrunch up my nose. I really need to learn some French. "Merci."

Stepping out of his van, I look around. There's a sign for the 'cascade', a popular local tourist spot, and literally nothing else. It's a mystical waterfall. I've seen adverts for it in the foyer of Linda and Bob's farm.

He drives off, probably wondering what on earth the crazy American woman is thinking, being out here in the middle of nowhere, alone. If it is any consolation to him, the crazy, American woman is thinking the same thing.

I take in my surroundings, trying to formulate a plan and decide to head for the waterfall. It is, after all, the only thing here. If I'm going to sit and contemplate my fate, I might as well do it in beautiful surroundings.

The walk takes a while, maybe half an hour, all downhill, but it is totally worth it. Fresh, clear mountain water gently drips from level to level, finishing with a pool of around thirty meters or so. All you can hear are the birds awakening and the rushing of the stream. They're right. It's truly a magical place.

At this time in the morning, with the sun peeking up over the mountain tops, there's not a single person around. I sit by the water's edge, take off my heels and let the surprisingly warm water soothe my aching toes.

What's my plan? Where am I going to go after this? I can't go home to LA. I'll surely be spotted, and my manager will be on my doorstep within the hour, battering down the door until she gets her own way. I have no desire to go back to G. Just thinking about him made me so mad. I can't even go visit my parents. Their absolute indifference at my existence is not the mood I need right now.

It looks like I'll have to stay here, by this enchanted pool, living off berries and leaves. It isn't the worst idea, as it's really quite stunning.

I unzip my dress, lay it by the side of the water and sink down into the pool before me, naked as the day I was born.

There's no forethought — how deep it'll be, whether a current is going to suck me down into a deep abyss, whether they have crocodiles in this part of France. All I know is that I desperately needed to plunge into that tempting water and swim until my troubles have dissipated into the stream.

This is my new home, after all.

I've been splashing around for a good thirty minutes or so when I hear voices. Slipping under the water, I swim under a tree that overhangs the corner of the pool and wait for them to leave.

They do precisely that, after a good twenty minutes, taking my dress with them as they go. *Fuck.* I've hidden my clutch under a small rock. I can see it peeking out from where I am crouched. Luckily you can't see it if you're just walking by. My phone and my wallet are safely hidden away from thieving visitors to my abode.

I repeat this dance for the next two hours, getting out when nobody is around then sinking back under the water as soon as somebody appears. My skin is getting pruney and, despite the heat of the sun rising above me, the chill of being in the water for so long is making me shiver.

As time goes on, storm clouds start to form overhead, chasing the tourists away. The sky darkens and distant rolls of thunder can be heard. Alone once again, I step out of the water and huddle against the rocks, shivering and afraid.

Regret is searing through my veins. I am alone – totally and utterly alone. Tears form in my eyes. My body shakes as hearty sobs rack my body. They will be heard by nobody. I am destined to die, naked, unloved and unwanted.

As the loud plops of rain fall onto the pool, a warm jacket envelops my shoulders. G scoops my weeping, shivering body up into his arms and carries me away.

He almost runs up to his car, cutting a good ten minutes off the walk as he hurries to get me somewhere safe. Placing me in the back seat, he lies down next to me and clutches my body to his until the trembling subsides.

"What were you thinking?" he asks as he holds my head to his chest, his warm arms enveloping me. "You could have died."

"I'm sorry," I whimper.

"No, I'm sorry. I let you down. I always let the people I love down."

I struggle to find the words. "How did you find me?"

"The caterer called my parents. He was worried about you. Not so worried that he dropped you off here, the asshole. I came as soon as I heard."

"My purse. I left my purse."

"Do you absolutely need it?" I lower my head. I don't *need* it, but my phone and my credit cards are in there. Okay I do need it a little. He sighs. "I'll go get it as soon as the storm subsides, and as soon as I know that you're all right."

"Why do you care?" I flash him an angry glare.

"Contrary to popular opinion" — he brushes his lips across mine, rubs our noses together — "I love you Sophie Smith." I kiss him back, savoring the familiarity of his embrace. I might hate him for what he'd said last night, but I also love him with all my heart.

It's no secret that I'm a total mess. *We've talked about this.*

Once he is reassured that I'm okay, he grabs a blanket from the trunk, wraps me in it and goes back in search of my purse. Then he drives me, in relative silence, back to his home. He doesn't touch me again.

After a shower and a hot meal, it is decided that I will return to LA. Well, I choose to leave and he reluctantly complies with my wishes. My embarrassment at the trouble I've caused and the unresolved differences between G and me are enough of a barrier to our relationship to make us both agree I am better off leaving.

It's not a solution that either of us want. I'm running away, like I always do when things get too complicated. He's closing off, like he did with Juliette. We're tearing ourselves apart because we simply don't know how to live, or love, any other way.

I sit on the bed crying as G packs my bag for me. He keeps insisting that I get under the covers and stay warm.

"I'm fine. I can do it." I say, tears streaming down my face.

"You're obviously not fine," he replies.

"I don't want to go back. They'll make me take the job."

He sits on the edge of the bed and grabs my foot as he speaks, then takes his hand away almost instantaneously, as if chastising himself for wanting to touch me. "Nobody can make you do anything you don't want to do. I thought all your talk about giving up acting was just holiday fever. I didn't realize that it was how you really felt."

I raise my hands. "It's all I talk about."

"I know." He sighs, a deep lung-emptying sigh that precedes the kind of speech nobody wants to hear. "I want to be the person you need right now, but I don't know if I can. I'm scared of making it worse. I have *so many* issues of my own that need to be dealt with. I had no idea just how being scared of committing to someone was ruining my life, until I met you."

I narrow my eyes. "The whole sleeping with your girlfriend's best friend didn't tip you off?"

He smiles. "I put it down to being young and stupid." He puts his hand back onto my foot, grasping on to it for dear life this time. "I really want it to work with you. You're...everything. But if that means going and getting some help, learning how to love, I need to do that first."

I crack, desperately trying to find something in the ashes of our relationship. "It doesn't have to be this way. We could do it together. I could stay, and we could work it out."

"No, you were right. I'm not the only one who needs to talk to someone, Shee. You need to figure out what's going on in your head, and you can't do that with me in your life. We're both trains in this train wreck, you and I, equally fucked to pieces."

He's not wrong. It doesn't make it hurt any less.

I let him finish packing my stuff while I sleep, then his brother drives me to the airport.

I get a last-minute place in economy, sandwiched between a screaming child and an elderly man who wants to tell me his life story.

I put my mask over my eyes and try to get some sleep. Tomorrow will bring new challenges and new fights. Without the love of a man or any kind of support system, will I succumb to the charms of the adoration of fans and the cocoon of the set? Will the temptation to re-find the acting family of my teens convince me to give up my longed-for freedom?

The answer is yes. When you're looking for love and companionship, sometimes you have to settle for what you're given.

Chapter Sixteen

September 30, 3 a.m.

Just this one job, I'd told her. Just this. Don't even think about booking me in for a single thing. The minute this is finished, I'm done.

The knock on the door is my signal that I am going to be needed in five minutes. It is three a.m. I put down my pen, stand up and stretch it out. Time to get out of study mode and back on set.

It knocks again, and the handle starts to open. I amble over and open the door.

"Hi." G stands on the steps of my trailer, scratching his head and looking at his feet, like he always did when he was nervous, in the 'before' time. My stomach does a little flip. He's still smoldering hot, even on a chilly Vancouver night.

"Hi."

What's he doing here? Why didn't he text me to say he was coming? I would have done my hair and maybe not looked like a sleep-deprived, overworked mess. I mean, that's a perfectly accurate description of me at the moment, but he doesn't need to know that. A little make-up does wonders.

I'd ghosted him after two-and-a-half weeks. The two a.m. declarations of love were too hard to handle. Not a word from him since.

He smiles. "Can I come in?" There's an awkwardness, as if we're ignoring our familiarity and pretending like we're just simple acquaintances.

I step back into the room. "Sure."

After three weeks, the celebrity gossip sites had declared us to be 'uncoupled'. I'm 'devastated' and G is 'already moving on.' "Did we...? Were we supposed to meet up?" *Why are you here?*

He shuffles his feet, hands in pockets. "I need the keys to the storage unit."

"Yes, of course. Sorry, of course you do." I turn around and rifle in my purse. "I've taken everything of mine out, so you know, we can cancel it when you've taken your stuff."

He nods. "Cool." He peers over my shoulder at the piles of books and papers on the table. "You working on something?"

"My GED, and an accounting and management course. Turns out I'm good at math. Who knew?" I giggle, nervously. "Ooh, and I learned to drive. Can you believe it?"

He smiles, visibly relaxing, and leans back against the wall. "That's awesome, Shee."

My stomach does another backflip when he says my name. I haven't heard that in a while. "And you? You're starting that indie movie, right?"

"Yeah. I start next week." He looks down at his feet—and the conversation stalls.

A million unsaid words float in the air.

I grab a sweatshirt and start putting it on. Exhaustion and the early morning chill are making me shiver. "And your family? They're good? And Tornado doesn't miss me too much, I hope?"

He shuffles some more, stubbing out an imaginary cigarette. "They're good. My parents were pretty mad at me, for…uh, letting you go."

"Gotta love Bob and Linda."

God, I missed them so much. They'd welcomed me into their home, treated me like one of the family, chores and all. G doesn't know how lucky he is to have them.

His eyes mist up, but he coughs and runs his hand through his hair so I won't see. The curls are even more unruly than they were this summer. They've gotten so long. I yearn to have the right to run my fingers through them one last time.

"Yeah. Tornado never got over you. His heart was broken into a million pieces when you left."

Are we still talking about Tornado?

"I miss him, too. Not a day goes by when I don't think about him." That was true for both of them.

"He didn't move on…with another llama. Those rumors aren't true." He steps forward. My hair is caught up in my hood, and he pulls it all out, brushing it out of my face, leaving his hand a little too long on the side of my head.

The sexual tension in the room shoots from hot to incendiary.

"Okay, well, I mean, if he had, that would be okay. I just want him to be happy." Lies, blatant lies. I want him to be as miserable and alone as I am.

He leans toward me, his nervous, rapid breath warm and welcome on my face. "I think you're the only woman he ever wanted."

"It could never work. A French llama and an American actress? People would talk." Our lips brush together with the very tips of our noses touching as I turn my head to one side.

My breath hitches, my mouth barely open, anticipating his kiss.

A loud knock sends us jumping back. "Five minutes, Sophie," a voice shouts through the door.

"I have to go," I say, turning and gathering my stuff.

"Sure, yeah, right." He holds up the key. "I'll get my stuff and return the key to the storage place. All done."

"All done."

"I guess I'll see you around." He opens the door and steps back outside, letting the cold night air into the room and dissipating any remaining heat.

"Yup." I shiver, rub the sides of my arms. "See you around."

Chapter Seventeen

October 10, 10 a.m.

"You'll be fine. It's just a promo thing, nothing special. Truth or dare, something like that." My manager has a very special way of convincing me to do something. It involves telling me it's 'just a little thing', when it's almost always three hours long and a complete nightmare. But I always do it anyway, because that's what Grandma would have wanted.

"It's just so awkward right now." It isn't even awkward. It's non-existent. Not a word from him since that day in the trailer, and that's how I want it to remain. My body and soul can't bear to be in his presence. To know he is in this world and not in my arms is hard enough to bear, but when he's right there in front of me, it's devastating.

Every time I see him it breaks anything I've mended. The shreds of my heart, finally melding together, are once again ripped apart.

"Some might suggest that you should have thought of that before you fell in love with your co-star."

Gee, thanks. Wise advice from my thrice-divorced manager.

"Oh my God, thank you, Suzy. That is so helpful, I didn't think to go back in time and change how I felt about someone."

I might occasionally use sarcasm as a defense mechanism. I'm working on it.

She sighs down the phone. "Just do it, please, Sophie."

I wash my hair and find something in my pile of 'free designer clothes for TV' that I keep for occasions like these. Honestly, since France, my wardrobe has been jeans and T-shirts, and I am not displeased with my new clothes. For a start, a casual outfit, teamed with scruffy hair and a pair of clear glasses makes me virtually unrecognizable. I sort of blend into the background.

New look. New, invisible me.

G is already there when I get to the studio. We're courteous, so he goes in for the hug. I oblige, then we head through to makeup and finally sit down in front of the camera.

"Hi, this is Gil…" I say.

"…And this is Sh— Sophie," he adds, almost fucking it up.

"And we're going to play ten things I didn't know about my co-star." We give each other serious side-eye then smile at the camera.

He pulls a question out of a glass fishbowl. "Something I do in my free time that I've never mentioned."

I point to myself. "Do I go first? Okay. I volunteer at a local animal refuge. I found out recently that I'm pretty good with animals, so I go whenever I can — walk the dogs, help clean out the stalls."

G tips his head to one side, his eyes glistening in admiration. "That is so cool. Uh, it's my turn. Mine is way less impressive. I took up yoga. I've spent some time recently in a retreat in Arizona, and one of the things we did was yoga every day, so I've kept it up. Gives me time to reflect in the morning."

What? Lost in his eyes, completely forgetting the cameras recording our every word, I ask, "You were in a retreat...in Arizona?"

He looks at the crew and back to me. "Yeah."

We're supposed to just answer the questions and move on, so I drop it, but I want to know more. *So much more.*

We carry on picking out questions. Favorite author, a song we know all the words to. Honestly, not a lot of it is a great surprise to either of us, but we make like it is for the camera.

"Ooh, this is a good one," I say picking out the last question. "If you could change anything about yourself, what would it be and why?"

"Oh, wow. I kind of hate my hair because it needs so much work, otherwise it's just a frizzy mess."

"Oh no, I love your hair." I forget myself for a second and lean forward, running my fingers through it. "It's so soft."

He licks his lips, gazes into my eyes. "Thank you." He takes the deepest breath and carries on. "I guess if I *had* to change something, it'd be to be less stuck in my ways. I'm a perfectionist and I kind of have to have everything in my life a certain way, you know? And life isn't *actually* like that. Plans can change. You don't have to be the person you thought you were going to be five years before, and that's okay, because maybe the person you are now is pretty cool." He sounds like my therapist. I'm going to need the number of that retreat.

I nod. "Wise advice, Gil." I hate calling him by that name. Does he feel the same way when he calls me Sophie? Breaking up sucks.

"I don't know what I'd change about me." I ponder the idea. There are a lot of things about my body that I hate, but nobody wants to hear how famous people don't like their looks.

He puts his hand on his heart. "You're perfect."

A flock of butterflies fly through my stomach. He still has it. He can still melt me with just the sound of his voice.

"Thank you." I wink at him. "I think I like the imperfect me. Is that a good answer? Like, despite what people think, I'm not perfect and that's okay. People fall in love with imperfect people every day."

He nods, a huge grin on his face. "They do."

Would it be bad if we made out, just a little, and got it out of our systems? No, there are at least three cameras pointed at us. *Damn it.* He's so hot right now, and I kind of want to tug on those curls a little.

"And you have to work on it, accept your faults and love yourself anyway." Now *I'm* sounding like my therapist.

We sit in awkward silence for a couple of seconds until someone shouts cut, then we do a couple of ten-second promo bits, and we're done.

"Arizona?" I ask as we wait to get our microphones removed.

"Therapy," he replies. "Understanding myself a little better."

I bounce up and down on my feet. This makes me so happy for him, for us. It gives me hope. "That's great. Although, with all your self-help knowledge, you probably taught them a thing or two."

"There was this woman, Elena, who was there at the same time as me. She was *so* into Tolle. It was cool to find someone who I could talk to about him, someone who shares the same philosophies."

I try as best as I can to keep my smile. "That's...nice." The sound guy finally arrives. "So, do you want to get something to eat maybe, after this?"

"Oh, I can't." In his defense, he looks genuinely disappointed. "I'm due back on set. I'm sorry. Another time?"

"Okay."

Stay. Don't leave me. Don't meet other interesting women. Love me. Come home with me and make love to me. "Another time."

Chapter Eighteen

October 31, 8 p.m.

I hadn't heard from Lucy since the beginning of August. I often comment on her social media but that's the limit of our interactions. So, when I got the invitation to her annual Halloween party, I ordered a costume and hopped on a plane.

It is nice to be back in LA for a few days. My house is cold and empty, but it's the nearest thing I have to a home.

Lucy lives only a few streets away from me, so I decide to walk to the party. There are kids everywhere, all dressed up, knocking on doors and running down the street after each other. It's a good time to be outside.

Lucy's house is beautifully decorated for the evening. This party is a staple event on the LA calendar, attracting the very best A-list stars. Nevertheless, she greets everybody at the door, like we're all one big rich, botoxed family getting together for the night.

"Oh my God, you look amazing." She's wearing the sexiest witch costume I've ever seen.

"I knew I wanted to be 'sexy something' but I didn't know what. Then I saw this and I knew I had to have it. You look pretty cute yourself," she replies.

I've gone for a pretty fairy costume. With hundreds of peacock feathers sewn into wings, it gives the most magical effect. I'd like to say I made it myself, but I've got exams coming up soon and I just didn't have the time.

I spot G's abs before I can even make out what his costume is. I can probably even recognize each one just by touch. The memory of gripping them is deeply etched into my brain. He's dressed as a half man, half beast. I approach, to get a closer look. The guy has *hooves*.

Is he 'llama man'? Is it bad that the idea of llama man gets me going just a little? Especially when the top half looks like that. *Eww.* I really needed to get laid.

The room is teeming with people talking loudly over each other and trying to get to either the bar on one side of the room or the buffet on the other. He glances over in my direction and lifts a hand, flashing me a timid smile. I should have known he'd be there. He and Lucy had become good friends while filming.

He is surrounded by beautiful women. The sight of him with no shirt on tends to have that effect. I point to the bar, and he excuses himself and heads in that direction too.

"Save me," he pleads, grabbing an orange cocktail.

I laugh at his desperation. "From what?"

"Women."

"All of them? That's going to take me some time. Plus, I am one. Do you need saving from me too?" *Be careful what you say here.*

"Never." *Good answer, Carter.*

"Shall we go outside?" We grab our drinks and head into the garden. The weather in LA is a drastic change to the chilly Canadian air. I've forgotten how much I love it here. "So, what are you?"

"Huh?" I point to his costume. "Oh, I'm Mr. Tumnus, a faun. It's from—"

"Narnia. Yeah, I love that book."

He flashes me a warm smile. "I know. So how are the studies going?"

I love that he has remembered, that he always takes such an interest in me. "Doing my GED in a few weeks, then my other exams are at the beginning of December, and I am done."

"Done?" He frowns, intrigued.

"Done with acting. Done with LA. I'm selling the house and heading for Europe. I thought I'd go llama hunting—for snuggles, hunting down llamas for snuggles." The sense of freedom that that gives me, the utter liberty to be able to say 'I have a plan' is joyful for me. Can he sense the positive energy that surges through me when I say it?

"Tornado would approve. Although, you know, you might have more luck if you went down south, to Peru." For the first time he hasn't balked or tried to dissuade me in any way.

I look at him, really soak him in. *God, I love this man.* I really need him to have changed if we have a hope in hell of working things out one day.

"So, are you seeing anyone?" I sip my drink, do my best to act nonchalant.

He shakes his head. "You?"

"Nope." We stand there in silence, contemplating, cogitating. "Want to go to my house and fuck?"

"Yep."

We run down those streets—as quickly as two people can, hindered by two goat's feet and a large pair of wings—skipping left and right to avoid the candy-laden kids.

I've hardly gotten the keycode in and shut the door behind us when G lifts me off my feet and slams my back against the wall, firmly planting his mouth on mine, the taste of his kiss sending shockwaves through me. My wings dig into my back and feathers fly everywhere, like confetti, but it's totally worth it.

His cock, hard and ready, pushes against me. I need his hot naked body on mine. I need to feel him inside of me.

This is so bad, so not how I'd imagined us getting back together, but it feels right too. Familiar. Home. If I'm going to be fucking anybody, I want it to be him.

"Let's take this upstairs," I say, pulling away from his kiss, delicious though it is. He drops me slowly, still pinning me against the wall, gives me the most devilish grin and takes my hand. "Lead the way."

In the most ridiculous sketch ever, it takes ten minutes to pull his hooves from his feet. "Are these things glued on?"

"No," he replies, tears of laughter streaming down his face. "They just fit really well."

Finally stripped down, he climbs over me and does that little backing away thing that he's always done, taking in my body.

"Still the same?" I bite my lip in anticipation. I've been busy working and studying, so haven't been to the gym as much as I should.

"I'd say it was just as I remembered, but honestly you're even more beautiful than that."

I grab his cock, wrap my fingers tightly around it. "Yeah, I didn't think it was possible either, but you got hotter too."

He gasps as I run my hand up and down his shaft, then brushes me away. "You first, then me." Dropping down between my thighs, he traces his warm, welcome tongue up my clit and gets to work making damn sure that I'm ready for him. He lifts his head. "Fuck, you're wet."

"I want you so bad. You can't even imagine." Climbing back up beside me and sinking his fingers deep in to my pussy, he watches my face as he does it.

"You want this?" His thumb circles my clit, flicking it back and forth as he goes.

Yes. All of that. Every single micro-touch.

I can't speak. I've waited so long for this, and now he's here, naked, in bed with me, making me come. I gasp and moan under his touch. My hips rise and sink with every caress. "I'm going to —"

My pussy tightens on his fingers, and he lands his lips on mine as I come for him. We're perfectly in sync, perfectly in touch with each other's bodies. He knows what I want, and he gives it to me.

He looks around. "Where do you keep your condoms?"

"In the bedside cabinet, but we don't need them, I mean, unless you've slept with anybody else since France."

His eyes twinkle with amusement "Of course not." He shakes his head, a coy smile forming on his lips. "No. So you're still on the pill?"

"Yeah." I gulp. "I never stopped, just in case — uh, in case this happened."

That earns me an even bigger smile.

We'd gone to a private clinic just before France and done tests, and I'd started taking the pill. The tests were clear, but the pill hadn't had time to take effect before I'd returned, so we'd never done it without a condom...until now.

He climbs over me, hovers over my pussy, pressing his cock against my clit. "So, you want to?"

"Yes. I've never done it without. Is it going to hurt?"

He pecks me on the lips. "No, Shee, it's going to blow your mind."

Fuck me, literally, he isn't wrong. The soft, silky smooth feeling of a naked cock inside me is a revelation. It's like eating a three-course meal in a classy restaurant when you've only consumed bread and water for your entire life.

I never want to stop doing this. I want to stay entwined with this man's body forever. From one to position to another, we get deeper and closer. My senses heightened, every nerve in my body is lit up like a fucking firework.

Sitting on the edge of the bed, facing him, I come gloriously, crying out and grinding into him, letting the waves ride through my body. He rolls me over, lifts my feet up by the ankles and pumps into me hard until he comes in me too, roaring loudly with triumph, his eyes closed, face red and pouring with sweat, as he empties himself inside me. Then he flops down onto my chest, utterly spent.

"Holy fuck," I whisper, trying to catch my breath.

"Holy fucking fuck," he says as he flops over next to me, laughing, and puts his hand to his chest. "That was..." I can't even find the words to describe it.

"A long time coming?" I snuggle up to him, playing with the little hairs on his chest, rubbing my hand up and down his taut stomach and savoring the fact that he is in my bed, in my arms.

He chuckles. "Yes."

We lie there in silence, allowing our bodies to come down from the euphoria.

"What are we doing?" he asks after a couple of minutes.

Oh shit.

Please welcome Guillaume Carter, otherwise known as 'The *Over*-Thinker'. They should make a statue in his honor.

"Thinking that I haven't eaten tonight and wondering what to order to get my strength back up for a second time?" I propose.

"I'm serious, Shee."

I know you are. I just don't want to have this conversation. Read the room, G.

"Fuck, G, let me enjoy this for five seconds without you telling me that you just want to be friends...*again*." My heart sinks.

"It's not that, I promise. It's just that I'm still in therapy and I'm still working things out." He sits up and moves to the edge of the bed.

"And that means what? That this was just a one-off, a step back when you should have gone forward." I sit behind him and run my hand down his back. I don't want to let him leave again, don't want my bed to be empty and cold.

"No. It means I'm not ready for commitment yet."

Holy fucking shitballs. "What?" It comes out a little louder, a little angrier than I'd intend it to.

"Shee, I love you. You're the only woman in my life. I'm not looking to meet anyone else and I'm praying that you'll wait for me, but I still need more time to work things out. I'm so close to being the man you need."

I grab on to him, wrap my arms tightly around him hold his body to mine. I am begging him. "You *are* everything I need."

He lifts my arms from his and stands. "But if I slip now, if I move too fast, I'm going to go back to being the man I was before, and I didn't like him, and you didn't deserve him."

I fall back on to the bed. "I don't know if I can keep doing this. You're breaking my heart."

He slides back toward me and wraps his arms around me. "No. I'm doing everything I can so I don't break it again."

Chapter Nineteen

November 22, 7 p.m.

In a twist of fate, like the knife that G stuck into my heart when he left in the early hours of the morning on Halloween and never called me again, our movie is an incredible success.

Only three-and-a-half months after we finished filming, our movie has been selected to open the Hollywood Directors' Society's annual festival.

Overly confident, the producers have rushed the editing and created a masterpiece. The few people who have seen it are calling it Oscar-worthy.

Well, shit. That put a huge spanner in the works as far as my plans to give up acting are concerned — and my plans to avoid G. All in all, it is the most terrible news I've had all year.

I am a rousing success, a lauded actress, with my face on a billboard in Times Square. Life sucks.

An invitation to the opening ceremony, the film premiere, followed by a private dinner with the producers plops onto my doormat and sends my world into overdrive.

My PA is flooded with offers of free dresses for me to wear on the night, my house fills with boxes and boxes of things people wanted me to promote and my manager books me interview after interview.

As the day comes around, I am teased and plucked and painted then squeezed into a corset inside the most beautiful dress. The only thing that is missing is someone to accompany me. I contemplated calling G — of course I did — but fear of rejection and a heart that hurts at just at the idea of hearing his voice prevents me from doing so.

My manager, insisting I be accompanied by someone, chooses Dylan, an actor on her books who is supposedly handsome and charming. He could be frickin' Jacob Elordi for all I care. He's just somebody to make it look like I am not a lonely old spinster — which, when you're a celebrity, is apparently a fate worse than death.

I called him and made it very clear that this is a friend doing a favor for a friend — no more, no less. I don't want him getting ideas.

"You look stunning," he says as he steps into the car that the producers have sent. "Ready for the red carpet."

"No. This is wild, right? I mean, what am I doing here?" *No really, can I go home now?*

"Getting what you deserve." Bless him, he might not be the man for me, but he is certainly a gentleman.

I deserve nothing. I've just done my job. I grasp Dylan's hand. "Thanks for doing this. I don't think I could have done any of this on my own."

He tightens his hand around mine. "My pleasure."

The car drops us off in front of the theater. Paparazzi and fans are lined up and the red carpet is literally right there, as soon as we step out of the car. "Let's do this," I say, throwing on my best, and widest, grin.

Dylan holds out his elbow, and I link my arm through his. We walk a few paces, stop to talk to a few fans, take a couple of selfies, then pose for the first set of photos.

Arriving at the front of the building, we wait our turn for the official photos and take a couple of minutes to breathe. Dylan is over-excited at being there. He hasn't ever done anything like this in his life and it shows. He is hyperventilating, in a good way, hopefully, and his face is frozen into a perfect, creepy grin.

"You're going to need to chill," I say, handing him a bottle of water from a table behind us. "Take a sip of that."

"This is it! This is fame." *Oh God. He thinks he's made it.* The guy has no idea how this works.

"When we move on to the next bit, you need to stand behind me while I answer questions and pose for the photographers. I'll call you over if I need you." It sounds harsh, but it's standard protocol.

The crowd roars behind us and two more people join the queue.

It's G and he has *Em* hanging off his arm.

Holy fuck. You have to be fucking kidding me.

My grip tightens on Dylan's arm, my heart rate goes up to a hundred and I do my very best not to let the world see how fucking furious I am.

Em. The girl who declared loud and clear that she was into G, like in *that* way.

"I'm not interested in anybody else," he'd said, and yet the minute my back is turned he's asked her to accompany him.

I turn away and compose myself. Has he seen me staring? Glaring? Losing my shit?

It is almost our turn. I pull Dylan down to ear level and whisper "You got this?" He nods in reply, and I let out a loud giggle and throw my head up as if he's just said the funniest thing I've ever heard, much to his confusion.

Worst acting of my life.

We step forward, and Dylan stays a few steps behind me as I start speaking to the queue of interviewers. I know some of the reporters. It always pays to try and remember a face or a name. People appreciate it, and you look like you care.

Not that I don't. I am really proud of this movie, as proud as I am of every acting job I've ever done. It is my whole life. I just don't care for this side of it — the publicity, the smarming. But this is my job, so I do what has to be done.

"Gil, come on over. Come join us," said the person I'm speaking to. *Shit.*

"Hi, Casey," says a familiar voice behind me. "Looking radiant tonight."

I can feel his hand hover above my lower back, a habit he doesn't seem to be able to rid himself of. The warmth of his fingers radiates through the thin material of my dress and surreptitiously slinks away when he corrects himself. I turn and look at him as he answers a question, my eyes darting up to his perfectly coiffed hair.

Fuck, he looks good. My insides do a little somersault. I forget where I am for a second as my body takes in the beauty of this man. My throat tightens, as the longing to kiss him, to touch him, engulfs me.

I put my hand to my mouth and cough it out, ever so quietly. *Pull yourself together, woman.*

As circumstance would have it, every single reporter wants to interview us together. It is no secret that early reviews have cited the 'incredible' chemistry between us.

They all want Sil...Gophie...*ugh*, I hope the fans have come up with something better than that. I'll google it later.

Little do they know that I want that, too — so bad that it hurts just to think about how much I want that hand on my back, those lips on mine. I jerk my head around to look at Dylan and smile. He and Em are patiently waiting, bless them. They look like lambs among the wolves.

After what seems like an eternity, we arrive at the end of the interview section. We pose for photos individually and together.

"You look beautiful," he whispers in my ear. "Can I put my arm around your waist for the photo?"

"Of course." I nod, tears forming in my eyes. He's made me cry with one simple sentence — because he cares enough to ask and because he has to ask because he isn't mine. He snakes his hand around my waist, sending a million messages to my brain that I choose to ignore, and pulls me in.

I look up at him and smile. His face fills with concern, spotting the tears. "We can do this," he says before releasing his grip, taking my hand and leading me away before the cameras spot my watery eyes. Once inside, we're faced with a large group of people, all vying for our attention—the crew and cast of the movie included. Em and Dylan catch up with us, and G gives my hand a final squeeze before letting it drop.

It's all so empty and cold without him, like when you know you've forgotten something. A sense of loss. Dylan is too excited to even notice that I've been crying, pulling me through the crowd and introducing himself to anybody who will listen.

"I need to powder my nose," I say, releasing my arm from his tight grip and heading for the bathroom.

Once inside, I place my hands on either side of the basin and look at myself in the mirror. "You've got this," I say to the empty room as I breathe in and out and calm my shit.

As if life hasn't thrown enough crap at me today, Em walks in, a face like thunder on her.

"I was looking for you," she snarls.

"You were?" I hate bitchiness between women. Hate it. I think back to Juliette and how amazing she was. I intend to show Em the same courtesy. I give her the best smile I can, given the circumstances, and the fact that she looks like she wants to kill me.

She smiles back at me, as condescendingly as she can manage. It wouldn't be in the spirit of female solidarity to suggest that she has so much botox and filler in her face that it is as frozen as a Disney queen's.

So, I won't do that.

"Don't get any ideas tonight, Soph. You've already stolen him from me once before, and I'm not going to let you do it again."

"What?" *I did* what *now?* She isn't making it easy for us to be best friends and bond over our mutual love of G.

She lifts a perfectly manicured finger and waves it under my nose. "The wrap party where you guys didn't even turn up. You knew I was going to make my move, and you got in there before me."

I let out a nervous chuckle. She's as intimidating as hell. "It wasn't like that at all. I didn't make G do anything he didn't already want to do." In fact, he'd wanted to do a ton of stuff that night, and, as far as I remember, I'd turned him down. *So, there.*

"Yeah, well, you had your chance, but he's mine now."

I have no answer to that. In my mind, he was always going to be mine, but maybe she's right, maybe I should let go.

He'd promised me the moon and the stars if I just waited for him. Perhaps he hasn't changed after all, and I've been stupidly hanging around for nothing. Better off alone than in bad company.

I smile at her. "Good luck." Heading out of the bathroom, I look for Dylan in the crowd, brushing past G as I go.

"You okay?"

"Great, fantastic, amazing. I've just been talking to your new girlfriend." I look back toward the bathroom as Em emerged. "You're perfect for each other."

I stomp off before he can reply, spotting Dylan on the stairs leading up to the theater. He's talking to my manager, Suzy, who throws me a 'save me' look, and I grab him and suggest we find our seats. She can't complain about having to listen to him drone on about this great idea he has for a movie. I've certainly heard enough of it in the car on the way here, and it was *her* suggestion that I bring him in the first place.

Of course, we're in the front row and of course I'm seated next to G. I try to pull the names off the chairs, but one of the organizers throws me a dirty look.

Cool, okay, I'll just leave them there.

We take our seats and wait for the room to fill. There's an opening speech by the President of the association, then our director does a little speech and the movie begins.

I haven't seen it. There was a screening at some point, but the idea of sitting through two hours of hot sex scenes with my ex-boyfriend didn't thrill me. It still doesn't.

The reviewers aren't wrong. The movie is great, and the chemistry between us is majorly hot. G's hand brushes my knee a couple of times during some of the most passionate scenes while Em sits there looking like she's chewing on a lemon.

Dylan just grins inanely and fidgets in his seat. He's probably itching to get to that dinner party where he can schmooze with some more big industry names. I've never felt so used.

The scene where our characters argue is particularly beautiful. G had come by my trailer beforehand, apologizing profusely in advance for the fact that he'd spend the day shouting at me. It made it so hard for me to be mad at him in those scenes, and that came across perfectly. You can tell we loved each other, even back then, when it was just wishful thinking on both our parts. It made for some incredible sexual tension.

When the movie finishes, the audience jumps to their feet in applause. G forgets himself for a second, whisking me into his arms and planting a huge kiss on my cheek.

"You don't ever need me to tell you how much of an amazing actress you are. You just proved it right there. Fucking hell, Shee, it was perfect."

"I couldn't have done it without you," I reply, detaching myself from him before the Rottweiler standing the other side of him attacks me. The rest of the cast and crew descend from all around us, and we become part of a giant hugfest. Even Dylan is right in there, hugging everybody as if he were in some way part of the movie, too.

A hand pulls me aside. "We need to talk," he says. "Are you dating Dylan?"

"Is it any business of yours if I am?" I reply.

"No, I just..." He breathes in through his nose, searching for the words. "I thought— No, you're right. None of my business." His face drops, as if his heart is breaking. Em drags him away, throwing me daggers over her shoulder as they leave.

This evening is horrible, which I'd kind of expected, but not at all for the reasons I'd imagined. I don't want to hurt G. I love him. *Why is this all so fucking hard?*

The dinner party is a small affair, just key cast members, crew and a few members of the association.

Dylan and I are seated at the opposite end of the table to G, thank God. I can't cope with any more drama. I have Lucy next to me, which is a bit odd, seeing as it is supposed to be 'boy, girl, boy, girl'.

"I think I complicated things by bringing a woman as my date," she says.

"Oh, I didn't realize that you—" I shut my mouth before I say something misplaced. I'm thrilled for her. I've only ever known Lucy to be single. I glance around her to see who the lucky lady is. She's seated next to an elderly woman of about eighty. To each their own, I guess.

"Oh!" She chokes on her wine and coughs into her glass, grabbing a serviette and coughing into it. "Not like that. I mean, not that I wouldn't, or haven't, but this was just someone I brought to make up the numbers. Arm candy, if you like."

I look over at Dylan, who has the breadbasket in his hand, inspecting the different rolls. "I get that." I wink at her, and she giggles.

"So, no more Gil then," she says, despondently. I shake my head. "Sorry to hear that. You made a great couple, on and off the screen."

"Yeah." My throat tightens. Honestly, I must spend half of my life holding back tears. It's been a tough few months—getting through my studies and working at the same time, my manager constantly on my back, trying to convince me not to give up my career, and I've finally cut ties with my family. Honestly, I'm not sure if they've even noticed. I've done all of it alone.

"Where is she, your arm candy?"

"Well, she should be sitting next to me, but she appears to be..." She looks over at G who is being fawned over, rather disgracefully. "Ah shit, sorry, Soph."

"*Em* is your plus one?" My jaw hits the floor. *You have to be kidding me. She wasn't his date?* "What the fuck?" Lucy's eighty-year-old neighbor lets out a squeak. I might have said that a little loud. I am perfectly justified. *What a bitch.*

Fuck The Sisterhood of the Traveling Gil. I want blood. Well, revenge. Well, you know, I want my G back, *damn it*.

The whole table turns to look, and I stare, steely eyed at Em. She pales, but in a final boost of confidence snuggles into G's shoulder. Bless him. G shrugs her off faster than a wet sock, finally clicking as to what's going on.

I have no idea what he says to her, but she sinks into the most ungraceful pose and stares into her wine glass, not even looking in my direction.

My G is still my G. He looks over at me and raises his hands in a 'what the fuck?' kind of way. I laugh, turn to Dylan, who is still puzzling over the bread, and throw a conspiratorial, 'save us' look right back at G.

We sit through four long courses of rich, carb-loaded meals and extremely dull, polite conversation, which seem to last several days, until we can finally sneak away.

I put my hand to his chest. "You're not dating Em?"

He kisses my forehead. "Fuck no. You're not dating Dylan?"

I giggle. "Please. Have you met him? Nice guy, but no way." I look down. "Em made me think you were together. I'm sorry. I was quick to jump to conclusions."

"No, it was my fault. She was all over me, and I saw you with him and thought, maybe you'd get a little jealous. That was about the dumbest thing I've done in my life."

"There was that time you —"

"No!"

I laugh, and he slips his hands around my waist, pushing me back against the wall.

"I miss you." He kisses my neck.

I sigh, the sigh of a thousand sorrows. "I miss you, too."

"I have to go away tomorrow morning. I'm filming right through until Christmas, then I'm supposed to be going home. Then I'm free for a while, if, you know, you want to get together."

Is he for real? Is it time? I don't want to get my hopes up.

"I'd like that. I have my GED, then other exams. I'm not free until Christmas either."

"This sucks. All I want to do right now is take you back to my place and do dirty things to you while we watch old movies and eat junk food."

I peck him on the lips. "You sure know how to seduce a woman."

He kisses me back. "It's one of my better qualities. I love you, Shee. I promise I'm worth the wait."

"I love you, too."

* * * *

November 22, 3 a.m.

It's 'Smarter'…our name. It was right there all along, Sophie Smith and Gil Carter. I'd get us T-shirts and stickers with it on them, but since we're not together anymore it's kind of redundant.

I ship-name us anyway.

Chapter Twenty

December 1, 3 p.m.

> *Sophie,*
> *I hope this email finds you well.*
> *I got your message about visiting in December. We would love to see you on the 17th.*
> *You're welcome to stay for Christmas. Guillaume will be joining us, and I'm sure he would love to see you.*
> *Bob will pick you up at the airport. Just send us the flight details,*
> *With love,*
> *Linda*
> *xxxx*

The invitation comes at the perfect time. I'd just started to look at where I'm going to visit in Europe when it flew into my inbox. Monica and Courtney started a text chain with me in it, and I mentioned my trip, so they insisted that I message their parents to see if I could come back and visit. Even Juliette is thrilled to be able to catch up. I'll be finished with my exams by then and just starting out on my journey of a lifetime.

I don't plan to stay on for Christmas. I thought I'd try out the ski slopes in the French Alps — or maybe Switzerland. I still don't know where I stand with G, and frankly, I'm no longer going to be available in January anyway. He'll be back to work somewhere, and I'll be off traveling. Perhaps fate is telling us that it was never meant to be.

It doesn't mean that I don't dream about him every night and wake up every morning wishing that he were lying there next to me, because I do...a lot, like to the point where I don't even want to fall asleep. But I can't spend my life pining for him. I have to move on.

I sent a courtesy text to G, in case he wasn't happy about it. It doesn't help with the whole 'moving on' thing, but I'm doing my best.

Hi, your sisters invited me to your parents' house in December, and I'm going on the 17th. I just wanted to check if that is okay with you.

Couldn't stay away from Tornado, huh? Give them a hug from me.

I will be giving them all the hugs, and I think we can all agree that it's Tornado who can't stay away from me.

I know that feeling well. Take Care. Miss you.

Miss you, too.

I do miss him. I miss him so much that it breaks me. A year ago, I never even knew he existed, and now, every day of my life is another day without him in it. How does that work? Why does fate throw these people into our lives and expect us to just get over it when they're gone?

I try to see the positive side of things. I quit acting, I'm nearly done with my education for the moment, and things are looking up. This year is going to end on the most positive note, and next year is going to be wild.

Chapter Twenty-One

December 17, 10:30 a.m.

Bob and Linda pick me up from the airport, obviously excited to see me. They wait for me to come to them, no pressure, but as soon as I open my arms, they go in for the hug. It's like I never left, like my heart isn't broken.

When we arrive, the table is laid and we sit right down to eat. The girls have prepared a wonderful meal, and we joke and catch up, talking about the movie, my plans and their love lives. The two of them are completely loved up with their French farmers, and I'm so happy for them.

After lunch, I trudge through the muddy snow to see my second favorite boy. The big old barns which had resounded with music and laughter in the summer months are now filled with straw and hay and all sorts of animals in pens. I wander through, petting the sheep and the three little pigs until I get to a corner stall and find my friend.

He's wary of me—I had, after all, abandoned him—but a few scritches under the ears, and he's happy to see me again.

"I've never seen anything like it," says Monica. "We got him from another farm. He'd been left to his own devices for a very long time and was in a bad way. We cleaned him up, but he never trusted humans again...until you came along."

This family has a habit of picking up strays. Even Tornado saw in me someone who had been rescued, too.

"I wish I could take him with me on my travels," I reply as I grab a carrot out of my bucket and feed it to him. He sniffs it, wary of hidden vitamins, then chomps away as soon as he's confident that no trickery is involved.

Warm stinky breath moistens my neck, and I turn to see, and smell, a large camel's mouth. "This is Daisy," says Courtney. "She's the camel dad picked up this summer. We had to isolate her for a while, to get her back up to health, and now we're slowly introducing her to the other animals. We'd hoped to put her in with the other llamas, but it doesn't seem to be working out that way. However"—Daisy pushes my head to one side, snakes around me and sniffs Tornado to see what I've done to him—"she does seem to have made one new friend."

Oh my God. Tornado has a girlfriend, and I am standing right between them, giving him snuggles and feeding him his favorite food. I sneak down and let the two of them do their snorty, sniffy thing.

"He's in love. That's so sweet." My heart is bursting with joy for my lonesome cowboy.

Monica looks at me like I've lost it. "She's a camel. They're from the same family of animals, but I don't think they mate or anything." She's very serious about the matter, but I'm already planning the wedding.

"Don't ruin this for me. It's the greatest love story of my life."

"Greater than yours and my brother's?" She smiles, teasing me.

"That's the saddest love story of my life," I reply, pinching my lips together. She pulls me in for a hug, and I hug her right back, even though she smells strongly of chicken poop.

"He loves you," she says into my ear.

"I know, but he isn't here with me, and he hasn't been for a long time." The constant boomerang of G's love has become tiresome. I'd wanted to see his family and the farm one last time before saying goodbye to these people. In France, you say *au revoir* and you say *adieu*. One means 'see you again' and the other really is goodbye. It is *adieu* to the Carter family after this stay. I need to move on from G, and this visit is the perfect way to sever all ties.

I've done it before, and I can do it again. Being alone.

* * * *

December 18, 8 a.m.

I'm in the bed that I shared with G, in his parent's house. I should get up, but I want to remember for a few minutes longer.

The sheets have been cleaned a dozen times since the summer, but it still feels like they have his smell on them — as if he's slept there all night and is in the bathroom getting his shave on.

Any minute now, he'll run back into the room, fold up his towel neatly and hang it over the radiator, then jump into bed with me, all cold from the shower, and soak up my warmth with his sweet-smelling body.

But it's December on the mountain, and even with the central heating, the room is cold and the bed even colder. I have thick fleecy pajamas and a hot water bottle, but the loft insulation is poor and there's snow on the roof.

The lack of warm hands wrapped around my body makes me shiver.

I shouldn't have come here.

* * * *

December 19, 8 p.m.

They reeled me in with their mountain and their snow, then they all went full family on me when I wasn't looking. Tonight, it's fondue, which involves dipping bits of bread into a melted cheese sauce and eating it with different charcuterie, followed by Christmas carols and hot chocolate with toppings in front of the fire.

"I've never had this," I say to Linda as we prepare the bread and charcuterie in the kitchen. She has had the Aga cooker burning all day to make the loaves, and the room is the toastiest place in the house.

She reaches over to the rack and grabs a bread knife. "What did you eat with your family when you were younger?"

"TV dinners or we ate out. Sunday lunch was always in a restaurant." I sink down onto a stool. "It wasn't like this. We wouldn't talk at the table, except for my parents who discussed grown-up things."

She turns to me and smiles. "I'm sure they still loved you, you know."

"Who?" I know who she means. I just don't believe it.

"Your parents," she replies, adding another glass of wine to her cheese sauce. "They fed and clothed you, brought you up with good manners and a good heart. That counts. Even if they didn't show you their love, they still cared."

I don't regret my childhood, nor do I hold my parents responsible for the fact that our family has fallen apart. Linda is right. In many ways, they did their best. It just didn't include any kind of emotional bonding.

I'd grown up with very few hugs, and it shows.

"Grandma had a lot to do with it as well, even if her love was conditional. She had a good, kind heart. She was a churchgoer, something my parents never believed in, and she was a great community person." Grandma had lost Grandpa very early in life, when my mom was only little. She hadn't married again. Between us and the church, she'd had very little else in life.

She sits down next to me, takes my hands in hers. "People express their love in different ways, but it's still love."

"Love languages," I reply. My favorite subject. She furrows her brow. "It's from a book."

"Oh right." She ponders the subject. "I wonder what mine is?"

"Acts of service. That's how you give love. And physical touch, like your son. G always has to be holding my hand or touching me in some way."

And I never minded, not one bit. Just like right now. I'd told my therapist about it, how these people had come into my life and performed some kind of magic. She'd just looked at me, as if to say, 'you know why', and we'd moved on to another of my problems.

Linda looked down at my hands in hers. "Wow, I never thought of it like that." She gives my hands a squeeze and lets go. Now that I've mentioned it, she is self-conscious, like when you think about the fact that you breathe, then you can't breathe without thinking about it.

"Yeah, it's funny, isn't it? But when you realize what makes the other person tick, it helps understand them better and improves your relationship. Well, in some cases." I laugh, embarrassed.

She tilts her head and looks me straight in the eyes. "He loves you, too, Sophie."

"So everybody keeps telling me." Is that why they invited me here? To try and convince me to get back together with G? Do they not know that it has never been me pushing this relationship away? Am I the bad guy in all this? I'm the one who walked away, sure, but, not through choice.

She steps back and starts cutting the bread again, as if she's wondering whether to continue talking. "He just needed time to get his head around things. He talks to me, you know. He told me he's seen you a couple of times."

"He did?" She knows about Halloween? I feel the blush rising in my cheeks.

"Oh, honey, he doesn't go into that much detail. I'm his mom," she adds, laughing. She stands up and grabs the large cauldron of cheesiness. "Let's get these people fed, huh?"

* * * *

December 21, 10 a.m.

Today is tobogganing with the grands. I'm on babysitting duty with Linda's precious little angels. She's dug out some old skiwear that has transported me back to a time when people wore fluorescent clothing with big old geometric shapes on it. I look like a Teletubby. Still comfortable, though, and super thick, which is a necessity considering the number of times I'm probably going to land on my butt.

G's nephews are blond and blue-eyed just like their father and grandmother. They have the energy of a small nuclear reactor, and they explode like one too, sometimes. When I'm not breaking up fights, I'm kissing 'ouchies' better and having to stop every five minutes while one of them writes their name in the snow...in yellow. That's 'the best'. I don't try it myself.

Tonight, is tree-trimming night. They've cut one down from the farm, and Bob has gotten out a huge pile of boxes of decorations from storage.

I reach into a box and pull out a beautiful glass angel. "This almost makes me wish I was staying for the big day," I say, regretting it instantly.

They all immediately insist that I absolutely can, and it wouldn't be a problem, but I give them my best, 'we all know why I'm going' look, and they drop it.

Except for Bob, who is fast becoming one of my favorite people. We'd hardly talked in the summer, he was so busy, but this time around I've got to know him better and can see why Linda is so enamored with her husband. He certainly is a charmer, if a little rustic at times.

He puts down the tree lights that he's been trying to untangle for forty minutes. "If it's because of my son and the fact that he dumped your ass, I wouldn't worry about that." Got to love Bob, always keeping it classy.

Linda throws him an angry mom stare. "Bob, please. I don't think she wants to talk about it."

"About the elephant in the room? Well, maybe we should. We let that boy down." He shakes his head. From the looks of it, what happened to us bothered him, and maybe what happened with Juliette. "He had the perfect woman right here, and we let him walk away because he's convinced the minute he falls in love it's going to make him miserable."

"It's their business, Bob," insists Linda. "It doesn't pay to get involved in your kids' business."

"I know, but we want to keep Sophie, don't we, guys?" They all nod and laugh. I shrug and raise my hands. What can you do? I love these guys. They'd been welcoming since the first day they'd met me, but I can't make G commit to me. That's not how it works.

All this is just going to make it harder to leave, and my plans for never seeing these guys again are fading fast. A couple of times I've almost packed my stuff up and gone. It would be easier that way. But I have plans to go out with Juliette and the twins tomorrow, and they'd be so disappointed. They're all treating me to a final night out.

Juliette hasn't stopped going on about her new boyfriend, a rugby player called Luc who is, apparently, a 'real Frenchman'. I assume that that is in comparison to a fake American one — and I have no idea what that means.

I'll be playing seventh wheel to the lot of them when we hit the local town. I've been promised drinks in a real French café-bar, then a restaurant with wine and fine dining. In my mind, I see checked tablecloths and a sultry piano player in a beret, accompanied by an accomplished ninety-year-old accordion player. There will also be cigarette smoke lingering in the air, even though it's been banned for years in France.

I have a feeling it's more likely to be plastic tablecloths and a TV in the corner of the bar, but I have my dreams of French rural life, and nothing is going to stop me.

Chapter Twenty-Two

December 22, 6:30 p.m.

It's officially my last day there. Only one more night until I leave for Paris. I am heading off on my first lone adventure, without a chaperone or a manager in sight. Nobody to keep me out of trouble. I'm so excited — and so completely terrified.

It will be an interesting experience, an exercise in restraint and tact. I'd made absolutely sure that Monica and Courtney were very clear on the fact that I didn't want to be set up with anybody tonight.

I kind of forgot to mention that to Juliette.

I'd told the twins that it was because I'm going traveling and don't want to be bothered with meeting new men. I certainly didn't want them to know that it's because I am still one hundred percent in love with their brother and waiting for the day that he turns up on my doorstep, declares his love for me once again and this time stays around long enough for coffee and eggs in the morning.

I've done an amazing job of convincing them, and myself, that I am quite happy on my own for now.

So, when we walk into the bar and discover the very delicious Luc and his even more delicious brother, another rugby player, my heart does a sort of semi-triple-jump. Like an 'oh my God that guy is gorgeous, and I want to jump him,' and at the same time feeling horribly guilty, cheaty and a very bad person.

I'd like to say that Matthieu, pronounced Mat-ee-uh, is rude or creepy or more interested in sports or other women than me, but it isn't the case. He is kind — like pulling your chair out for you, paying for your drink, complimenting you constantly but in a really smart and not a demeaning way kind of kind — and he is funny, and he is hot.

And, you know what? It makes me feel good. I haven't had a lot of attention from someone of the male persuasion in quite a while. I've been busy studying, and the few times I've seen G have been fraught with emotion and not at all relaxing or fun.

Well, there was Halloween. We'll always have Halloween.

Oh, Halloween.

Just thinking about it makes me get all emotional. And yes, I do mean in my panties.

So, my head isn't turned, nor my heart, but it's a pleasant night out, so I go along with it.

The twins, however, see red. Firstly, because I've insisted on not wanting to meet anybody, and secondly, because, as we all know, his entire family wants me to get back with G.

"So, tell me, Sophie. You have a new movie coming out soon?" asks Mathieu, leaning right in to hear my reply. The bar isn't busy, and we're all seated closely together. There really is no need for such suggestive leaning.

Courtney harrumphs, loudly.

"Starring our brother too. He stars in it with her. It's a love story and there are a lot of sex scenes," says Monica, curtly.

I balk. She makes it sound so dirty. "Well, I wouldn't say a lot. It's not porn or anything. They're considering it for the Oscars."

Matthieu's eyes widen. "The Oscars, eh? So, you are a big star in Hollywood. I don't watch too much TV and movies. I like to read." He shrugs it off as if TV and movies are beneath him.

"You like to read?" I do like a man who gets lost in a good book. *Like G,* I remind myself. *He likes to read, too. Stop getting distracted by this man's beautiful eyes and remember the goal here.*

"You know who else likes to read? My brother." It's as if Courtney has read my mind.

Matthieu nods, pauses for a second and turns to look at the twins. "Your brother is the man who sleeps with Juliette's best friend then tries to sleep with Juliette when he is with Sophie, yes?"

Monica gasps and turns puce. "Yes. But—"

Matthieu sighs. "I don't want to talk about your brother. I want to talk about Sophie." He turns back to look at me.

Burn.

"Oh God, I don't want to be the subject of any conversation." I wave my hands. "Talk about something else. Luc, Matthieu, tell me about your jobs.

Do you play for the same team? Rugby is like American football, right?" This causes one brother to whistle loudly in disagreement, and the other men at the table to throw back their heads with laughter and tap the table so hard that it almost falls over.

"This is a joke?" asks Matthieu. "It's not a joke? There are American footballers and there are rugby players. Real men." What is it that these guys have with this 'real man', thing?

"You see this?" Luc leans forward and shows me a large scar running across his head from ear to ear. "I did this in the final last year. I say to the medic 'staple it', you know? Clack, clack, clack. Then he puts on…uh…a bandage and, *bam*, I go out and I play the rest of game. No helmets, no pads on my arms. A *real* man."

Ah, okay, well, yeah, I guess that's one way of calling it.

The twins are visibly agitated by the whole 'Matthieu' situation, and, at their suggestion, we head out into the cold night to the restaurant, only a few streets away. It's winter and it's supposed to be cold, but the thing is, it seems a little whiter and a lot chillier than when we'd arrived a few hours earlier.

Juliette gets out her phone. "They didn't say snow for tonight. It snows tomorrow."

"Is it bad?" There are already several inches of snow, and I have to get to the train station tomorrow, which is a good three-quarters of an hour away by car from G's parents' house. *It'll be fine, right?*

We trudge to the restaurant, and I'm seated as far away from Matthieu as is humanly possible, thanks to my self-designated bodyguards.

God forbid I'll lose all my control around him and jump him on the table over the *foie gras* and oysters.

The restaurant appears to be run by the same man who was sucking Linda's face at Bob's party, so we're given the best table and the best service. Obviously, the twins have a hand in it. There has to be benefits to your parents taking lovers. The wine changes with every course as well—sweet white for the starter, then red, then champagne with the dessert. We must have been sat here for three hours at least.

As we're finishing our dessert, a creamy chocolate delight, the waiter comes over and announces something to our table. "No time for coffee. We have to go," says Juliette. "He says they close early tonight, because of the snow."

I look outside. *Fuck.* The snow is really deep. "Are we going to be able to get home?"

The farm boys laugh and say that their truck can get through anything, and if it doesn't, their dad will bring the tractor down and pick us up. Juliette pales, though. They lived a good hour away and it doesn't look like Luc's fancy Mercedes is going to get through this stuff.

"Looks like we're staying with you tonight," said Matthieu, with a wink, as everybody jabbers away in French, gets their phones out, calls parents and arranges everything.

Oh God. I'm not sure I can cope with G's family and their protective instinct on top of Matthieu and his seductive charm. The whole situation is getting a little stressful. I thank all the gods that G hasn't arrived yet, because, honestly, I cannot cope.

Back at the house, a chain of protection is put around me by everybody except Linda, who finds the whole situation absolutely hilarious and who suggests I 'get in there' if I want to, and if I don't, would I mind if she does?

Good God. The woman is unstoppable.

She serves us hot chocolates and makes up beds for everybody. The twins will bunk together, the two brothers will sleep in the room made available as a result and I'll share with Juliette.

I imagine G arriving early, coming upstairs and slipping into his bed to find me, then reaching over and finding his ex. I can also imagine Luc's face if that happened.

It would definitely be best for all if we all stayed in our rooms tonight, for my sanity, if not for the sanity of those around me.

Chapter Twenty-Three

December 23, 8:30 a.m.

There's nothing like breakfast in bed, and what Luc and Matthieu bring to our room at the ungodly hour of eight a.m. is, indeed, nothing like breakfast in bed. There may be muesli or granola or it might be oats with some kind of fruit and goat's milk. The texture is mushy but with a twist of a crunch. I won't be repeating the experience. Juliette laps it up then she laps up Luc, in a kissy way, on the bed next to me. That's pretty mushy too.

Matthieu leans on the doorway, his arms crossed, looking smooth.

"I hate to throw you all out, but I'm leaving today, so I'm going to need to pack," I announce.

"You're going?" asks Matthieu. "You don't stay for Christmas?" He looks almost disappointed, as if he is staying for Christmas too.

"She's not going anywhere," says a familiar voice from behind him. "The trains are cancelled, as are the flights. I got the last one in." Matthieu is unceremoniously pushed aside as G enters the room. He grimaces at the sight of Luc and Juliette, the same face I'd made when I'd eaten the goat's milk concoction.

"Guillaume!" exclaims Juliette, detaching Luc from her mouth and pulling up the sheets.

He throws her a fake smile then turns to me, his eyes lighting up. "Should I ask why you're having an orgy — or have you just been spending a little too much time with my family?"

"None of these people are mine," I reply.

Matthieu makes a 'hmm' sound, as if to insinuate that I could be his. I swear, G's head spins a hundred and eighty degrees. The look on his face... He does not like that one bit.

Matthieu, the six-foot-something rugby player shrinks several feet. Strong and sturdy he might be, but at this precise moment, faced with G's wrath, he looks about two inches tall.

"Ladies, Gentlemen, I'm going to have to ask you all to leave. Train or not, I am going to have to get up from my bed eventually. That includes you, Mr. Carter." G's head spins back around. Him? He'll have to leave too? *Damn right.*

He isn't going to weasel his way back in like he's done every other time. If there's one thing that meeting Matthieu has taught me is that I deserve to be wooed, seduced and charmed a little. I am not going to welcome him back into my bed just like that.

Between us, I'm not going to make him wait that long, either, because even after a twelve-hour flight, the man looks like a fucking god. I have my standards, but I am also, you know, a little horny for some G.

Some D.

G's D.

Juliette takes Luc's hand, and they go off to find somewhere warm and discrete. G brushes past his nemesis, again, almost knocking him over, and storms downstairs. Matthieu winks at me and smiles. I shake my head, laughing, and shoo him away. He has guts. I have to give him that.

I lock the door, take a shower and make myself as gorgeous as I can, considering that I have to dress for the cold. I go for the oversized jumper, skinny jeans look. Hopefully it makes me look cute and snuggly.

I also opt for the expensive perfume. I hadn't planned on bringing it, then I'd popped it in my suitcase at the last minute as a 'you never know' backup. *Thank you, past-me, for your foresight.*

I waft down the stairs and into the kitchen, ready to face everybody, only to discover that there's nobody there except Linda, who I am starting to believe has been secretly chained to the stove.

Blink twice if you need rescuing.

"Where are they all?"

"Bunch of randy, hormone-filled doohickeys. I sent them all to do chores. You look gorgeous today and you smell…expensive. I imagine you've already spoken to my Guillaume?"

I smirk. "Thank you. Yes, I have."

"We don't play games in this house, Missy." She waves her finger at me, scowling, before cracking a smile. "But it doesn't hurt the cat to chase the mouse a little before it gets its supper."

I help her prepare lunch for our extra guests and go off in search of Bob, who is going to give me the lowdown on whether I am actually going to leave today…or ever. Maybe I'll just move in and spend the rest of my life baking with Linda and feeding carrots to Tornado.

It wouldn't be the worst thing that has ever happened to me.

"I'm sorry, Soph. Even if they clear the roads, they've cancelled all the TGVs. You're not going anywhere tonight. Plus, they're predicting even more snow tonight and tomorrow. The lads and I are going to go get Luc's car dug out this afternoon, so they'll be able to get home if they stick to the bigger roads. Looks like you're here for Christmas after all."

"If I didn't know better, I'd say you planned this."

"Honey, as a farmer, I'd like nothing more than to control the weather." He shoos me away. "Now get back inside before the cold seeps through that thin California skin of yours."

"I'm fine." I say, through chattering teeth.

He roars with laughter. "You're shivering like a Chihuahua with a fever."

We ring the bell for lunch at midday, and everybody trudges back in. They peel off their wet coats and boots and prepare to eat a hearty meal before going down to town in Bob's tractor to dig out the car.

"Can I help with anything?" asks Matthieu. I've already laid the table and am almost finished with carrying the bowls of food through to the dining room. It's difficult to tell whether he genuinely wants to help or whether this is one-upmanship with G.

Whatever his intentions, the already taut atmosphere in the room gets a little more so. "No, thank you, I've got this," I reply. "Take a seat. Help yourselves, guys."

"You're not going to join us?" asks G, tapping the empty seat beside him and throwing a sly smile at Matthieu.

The National Guard — comprising of two overbearing sisters and one reluctant brother — have already made it so that Matthieu is seated with Luc and Juliette and the only seat left is next to G.

I smile. "Just a minute. I haven't finished bringing everything through."

"Then I can help," adds Matthieu, who goes to get up.

"Sit down!" choruses the sisters. He shrugs his shoulders and sits again, chuckling to himself. He's built like a tank, but he is as soft as a teddy bear — or so it seems.

"Don't be rude. He's only offering to help, which is more than I can say for the rest of you." I look at the girls in the same way Linda looked at me earlier, and they balk and apologize.

This is fun. Well, not for poor Matthieu, who either can't read the room or is so determined to get my number that he'll risk life and limb. It's a whole lot of fun, until it isn't — until it goes all kinds of sideways and then some.

I head back to the kitchen to get the rest of the food. "Can you pop out back to the pantry and get a couple of bottles of fizzy water? The nice stuff," asked Linda.

"Sure."

I bend over to pull the bottles out of the wine rack and feel a warm hand grab onto my butt. I swat it away, turn to tell G that he can't just walk back in and assume I'll be all over and him.

But it isn't G.

I fly back into Linda and Bob's precious wine collection — dislodging a couple of reds, but not causing any actual damage, thankfully — when I'm faced with Matthieu's giant chest.

I hold up the plastic water bottles in front of me to make a barrier between us. "Fuck off!"

He shrugs, grinning like an idiot, then raises his hands like he is being arrested. "Who could resist?"

I do the thing that women do, the de-escalation of a situation. "I'm sorry if I haven't been clear, but I'm not interested." I'm not sorry. I just don't want him to touch me again.

"Are you sure?" he insists, taking another step forward and opening his arms for me to jump into.

"Very." *Okay, now he's pissing me off.*

As if his behavior is in any way appropriate... Even if I *were* interested, even though I thought I'd made it pretty clear that I'm not, this is never acceptable. Men are a complete mystery to me.

"Then you take a selfie with me? You're a celebrity, so I'll get likes." *What the fuck? You have to be kidding me.*

He can't have me, so he'll just use me for likes.

Fuck. I had such high hopes for Matthieu, but with every move he's made today he's just disappointed me further and further. I give in...if it'll get rid of him.

"I guess." I pick up the water bottles and wait for him to move. "Well, not here." I want to be in the kitchen with Linda...or with G. Anywhere but this little room. Alone.

But he doesn't move, just pulls out his phone and fiddles with it.

"Let me pass." I stay fixed to the spot. I don't want to have to squeeze through the doorway that he is filling. Any attraction I've found in this man is slowly dissolving into disgust as the seconds pass.

"You heard her." I'd like to say I don't need G to rescue me, but my heart is racing, and I am starting to feel a little dizzy.

Sometimes a little backup is a good thing.

"Okay, okay. We take a little selfie is all." Matthieu raises his hands again as though we're the ones being rude. He steps aside to allow me out, and just as I walked past him, he wraps his arm around my neck — not even my shoulders but a full throat hold.

G's eyes look like they're going to pop out of his head. He is raging.

"Let go of her! *Now!*"

My mind is racing. *Breathe, just breathe*. He'll take the photo and let you go.

Matthieu holds up the phone and takes a selfie, putting his head down next to mine. It has to be the worst photo of me ever, my face red and terrified from the tight arm pushing against my throat.

"I'm going to give you three seconds to let go of Sophie and hand me your phone." Linda stands behind G, her rolling pin in hand.

"Whoa, *on se calme, la!*" Matthieu reverts to French, letting go of me and sulking, hands in pockets, as if we're all a bunch of annoying nags and he's done nothing wrong.

I fall into G's arms — partly because I need to be held and partly because his fists are rolled up so tightly, I'm afraid that the minute Matthieu let me go he'd punch him. While I'd loved to have seen that, I'm pretty sure Goliath would have socked him back harder.

I've had my fill of 'real men' and am quite happy to be in the arms of my sweet G.

"Phone," repeats Linda.

Matthieu hands it over and she passes it back to Monica and Courtney, who delete the photo. Then Luc literally pulls his brother out of the kitchen by his shirt sleeves. He is raging, too.

G sits me down at the kitchen table and crouches down in front of me, placing his hands ever so gently on the chair at either side of my knees.

"You okay?" His face is filled with worry.

I take a few deep breaths. "I'm fine. I'm sorry for all this fuss."

"Shee, you have nothing to be sorry about. I never realized how…invasive it is. I mean, I know you told me but, fuck, these guys treat you like a piece of meat."

"It was different. I think I gave him the wrong message." I am consumed with guilt. If I hadn't been so nice to him, so flirty… If I'd just made it clear that I am not interested.

"Stop defending him."

"I know. I know." His face is only inches from mine, and I just want to kiss him and fall back into his arms. But we're in his mom's kitchen and the food is on the table getting cold, and I don't want this whole situation to be a thing anymore because it is always a thing with me, and it makes me feel like some kind of diva. "I want to kiss you, but I can't."

He lowers his gaze to my mouth and moistens his lips. "I get it. You need time."

"I do. I need time to think about what being here with you means, and we need to just talk, you know. I'm going to be gone in a couple of days. I can't just do the thing where I let you back in, then it all goes wrong again."

"It's fine. Just so you know where we stand, I want to kiss you too."

Don't say that. Jeez, G, I 'm biting my tongue so hard it's gone numb.

I lean my face right up close to his and breathe him in a little, like when your grandma bakes a pie and you're not allowed to eat. It smells delicious, so you just waft your head over it and smell it a bit, imagining how good it's going to taste when it's in your mouth.

That will do for today. Just a hint of a taste.

I have to protect my fast-beating heart.

Chapter Twenty-Four

G wanted me to eat in the kitchen, but I go back into the dining room. I want Matthieu to see that he doesn't intimidate me. It's a lie. I'm in a terrible state, but I make it through the meal alive.

Lunch is a somber affair, followed by hugs with Juliette, then all the boys leave to free their car and get home. I feel bad for Luc and Juliette, who've been so sweet and apologetic. Matthieu has been silenced by his brother — under threat of I don't know what, but it works. He doesn't speak to me again.

G heads up for a nap. He's exhausted.

Bob's cousin and his wife are coming for Christmas, with their young daughter. Linda is busy washing and drying bedsheets and preparing the rooms.

"I have something to ask you," she says, embarrassed.

"Do I need to book a room in a hotel? I totally get it."

"Well, it's not that, exactly. I spoke to G this morning and he's, uh, he's happy for you to stay in his room. We'll get the put-you-up out of storage. You don't have to share a bed. Is that something you think you can do? We'd really like you to stay and join in all of the festivities."

"Will there be warm cookies?"

"So many warm cookies," she smiles and places her hand on the side of my head, just like G always does. "I'd feel better if you were here with us and, you know, you're starting to feel like a member of the family. A hugely dysfunctional family, but a family nonetheless."

"I'll have any family that takes me, if there are cookies," I reply. "Even this crazy one."

"Hey," she says, chuckling, "I'm the only one allowed to call them crazy." She ruffles my hair, and I help her with the washing. I'll have to be careful. All this cooking and housework. People will talk. I have a reputation to keep up.

Everybody arrives at once. Bob's family have followed his snowplow up to the house. Their little girl is only three and is just a delight. She is waiting for *Pere Noel* with great excitement. She thinks our tree is the most beautiful thing she has ever seen.

Our tree? If past me could hear me right now she'd be like, '*What? Who is this woman?*' Celebrating Christmas like a frickin' family member. Wild.

The grands turn up, too, and Linda settles them all down with popcorn and Disney movies. It is going to be a long few days for these little guys.

Some of the grown-ups get into boots and fluorescent ski-gear and go for a walk in the snow. I sneak upstairs and shimmy like a commando across my bed to get to G.

I ruffle the tufts of hair that are sticking out of the top of the sheets. "You asleep?"

He pops his head out. "No. You want to join me?"

A little giggly snort comes out of my nose. "No, silly, I want you to come for a walk with me before it gets too dark."

He lifts his head, his eyes half-closed. "What time is it?"

"Time to go for a walk."

He sighs and sits up, letting the sheet drop to reveal *those* abs. Admittedly, they're scrunched up as he hunches forward, scratching his head and yawning, but they're still perfectly beautiful.

"Give me a second to wake up." He turns to look at me. "Are you checking me out?"

"No...maybe."

A smile creeps onto his face. "You sure you don't want that kiss?"

"No. I want to build a snowman." He rolls his eyes, signals at me to look away and gets out of bed. I make a big deal of sticking my hands over my eyes.

"No peeking." He chuckles at my silliness and throws his clothes on. "You sure you want to sleep in the z-bed tonight? It's pretty lethal. Several friends and family have almost lost their lives in it when it has snapped up unexpectedly."

I shake my head. "I'll take my chances." *What other option is there, huh? His bed? Nuh-uh. I'm not falling for that one.*

He shrugs. "I'm just saying."

The farm and the surrounding countryside are beautiful in the snow — just endless waves of white as far as the eye can see. The sky above is gray. More snowstorms are due tonight, and G's dad has stocked up on wood to keep the fire burning. It looks like Christmas is definitely going to be an indoor affair and that I am most definitely going to be present for it.

I haven't picked up my phone in days, except for a couple of texts to Juliette. I have hardly been online at all, either. My days are so busy, and I'm so tired at night. The fresh mountain air is doing wonders for my sleep pattern.

"You've had a stupid grin on your face for ten minutes now. What are you thinking about? Is it my abs? It's my abs, isn't it?" Even through ten layers of clothing, I can feel G's hand on my back.

I don't mind. It feels like home. I like it like that.

"I'm thinking about how happy I am, which is making me happier."

"I'm happy you're happy. I'd be happier if I was part of that happy."

"You are, in a way—being here, with you, in this magical winter wonderland, and your family. That's all I need right now. I know it won't last, and I know I'm going away as soon as all this cold, white stuff allows me to, but for now—just right now—this is perfect."

His face drops. "Okay."

"It's not because I don't want to and not because I don't love you, but because it won't last. And if I give in to the physical feelings, my emotions will get involved too and I won't be happy anymore," I explain.

"Boundaries then. That's what you're saying." He drops his hand.

I turn and grab hold of it, putting it back. "Separate beds and no kissing, but reassuring touches and snuggles are good."

"Snuggles sound great."

They sound perfect. My happy just got happier.

"Not naked snuggles," I added with a wink. "Just friendly ones."

He laughs. "Clothes. Got it. Right."

"Sleeping in pajamas would be a good start." Expecting a sarcastic quip in return, I get nothing. In fact, when I turned to see if he agrees, he has completely disappeared.

What?

I look around to see if he's sunk into a snowdrift and is being dragged away by wolves — I've feared just this thing having seen too many animated kids' movies set in Europe — but when a hard lump of the cold, wet stuff thwacks into the top of my beanie, I realized that war has been declared.

I bend down, grab a handful of snow to defend myself and try to spot him, but another missile goes flying over my shoulder and slams into the back of Bob's head before I can find G.

"I'm hit. Save yourselves!" cries Bob. Then he flings himself to the ground dramatically and starts rolling his own ammo.

It is a snowball fight, and I am slap bang in the middle of it, getting hit from all directions.

This is happy. This is how happy feels and it's wonderful.

* * * *

December 23, 4:30 p.m.

After the snowball fight — which ended in the sad demise of Bob's beanie when it flew off into a drift and was never seen again, we return home.

A fresh batch of Linda's special hot chocolate, containing around seventy percent bourbon, steams in mugs on the counter. Nobody's cold after a sip of that. In fact, I no longer feel much of anything except the desire to down another one.

Everyone settles in to play board games with the kids, and G and I sneak upstairs for a chat.

"Don't sit on it," says G, as I lower my butt down onto the put-you-up. "It'll fold right up on you."

"You're starting to worry me about sleeping in this thing." At first, I was sure it was a ploy, but the more he insists, the more I'm starting to wonder if he's actually just looking out for my interests.

"I told you, it's a death trap. You're more than welcome to sleep in the bed with me."

"I can't." I can't resist him. I can't stop myself from wanting to ravage him, take him, hold him in my arms and do stuff with him that makes the bed squeak.

He grabs his infamous messenger bag, puts it on the bed and rifles around in it. "I won't do anything. You're quite safe."

It isn't him I'm worried about.

"I know you won't." I sit down on the bed and get comfortable. "I trust you. I'm not sure I trust me."

He smiles, pleased with himself. Must be nice to know women can't resist you.

"So."

"So?"

"I brought you something. It's not your Christmas present, though. I saw it in a shop and thought of you." He pulls out a little silk bag.

I take the little bag and empty the contents into my hand. It's a silver necklace with a llama charm hanging from it. "Oh my God, that's so sweet."

"Now you can take Tornado with you wherever you go." He lifts his hand to the side of my head but recoils—maybe thinking better of it. "I've heard he's moved on from you to someone a little more…four-legged, but seeing as he was your first love, I thought you'd appreciate it."

It's the sweetest thing anybody has ever given me. I lean over and peck him on the lips. Just a quick kiss, to say thank you. "He wasn't my first love."

"He wasn't?" My lips hover over his. I want to pull back but I stay there, our faces only a breath apart, trying to resist. Just one little kiss won't hurt, right?

I place my lips back on his.

He doesn't react, seemingly nervous of my intentions. "This is where you kiss me," I say, my lips smooshed against his. He unleashes a kiss that I wasn't expecting—passionate, hungry.

Sticking his hand behind my head, he lays us down on the mattress, his mouth still on mine, like the movie hero that he is. Slick and sexy.

My body is screaming for more. The one thing I've been avoiding is happening and yet I want it more than anything in the world. It is intense, hard—his lips on mine, his body pressed against me, a million missed kisses in one.

It goes on for what seems like hours. Sometimes he'll stop and just look at me, his hand still firmly gripping my head, his body, hard and ready, glued to mine. He doesn't try to touch me, undress me or kiss me anywhere else. His focus is solely and uniquely on this kiss. His respect for me holds back his clear desire for more.

"I feel like a teenager again," he jokes as he pulled away from me. "French kissing in my French bedroom.

If I'd known that was your reaction when I bought you jewelry, I'd have showered you with it months ago."

I raise my eyebrows. "You might have gotten it thrown back in your face."

He smiles. Maybe it's the adrenaline or whatever hormones are racing through my body right now, but he looks freakishly handsome, hovering over me, his dark curls falling down over his forehead. "Probably."

"I want to be with you," I say.

"I want to be with you too. But you're leaving. And you think I'm leaving too." I *know* he's leaving. Sooner or later he'll go back to LA or Canada, and I will be alone.

I trace a finger down his chest. "You *are* going to leave, though."

"That kind of depends on you…on what you want." *Oh no, don't make it up to me.*

I shake my head. "No. What about what *you* want?"

"I want to be with you." He kisses me again, a kiss filled with hope and longing.

I can't be the one to decide whether we should be together. The opportunities that are going to come G's way after the success of our movie are everything he's worked for. I can't live with making him walk away from that.

I put a hand on his cheek and closed my eyes, touching a face I've only seen in my memories for what seems like forever. "I'm not going back," I say. "My home is sold, and my stuff's in storage. I'm going to spend this year working on a business plan, then — when I'm ready — I'm going to live somewhere in this world that makes me happy and do something that pleases me — probably from home. There will most likely be dogs and cats in this home — and comfortable clothes and no make-up. I just want to be clear that that's what you'll be signing up for."

He doesn't flinch or balk or do any of the things I would have expected him to do. "Anything else?"

"No. I'm not looking for marriage or kids or promises of eternity together. It's not that I don't want that. It's just that that happens naturally, when you're ready, not on demand."

He nodded. "Okay." His face is pensive. I know I'm being selfish. The Sophie in front of him isn't the Sophie he'd fallen in love with, and I'd realized, with the help of Dr. K, that our break-up was as much my fault as it was his.

I blamed him for being commitment-phobic, but I'd thrown him for a loop with my intention to give up acting — and that wasn't fair.

The only way to move forward was for both of us to be honest about exactly what we wanted — and stick to it.

"What do you really want, though? From life, not just now?" I ask.

He rolls down beside me, onto his back. "You know what? I want to be as happy as you were in the snow. I want to make more movies, I want to read all the books I can, especially the ones that help me a better person, and I want to meet Eckhart Tolle."

I let out a laugh. "You'd scare him away with how much of a fan of him you are."

He turns to look at me. "Oh my God, can you imagine? I'd be a wreck."

We agree that we both need time to think. And that the kissing should stop — it probably won't — and that we'll build a fort of pillows between us tonight so that

I can sleep in the bed and not be tempted by G's delicious body.

He seems genuinely able to restrain himself around me, which is disappointing, but I console myself in the fact that he's a really good actor, so he's probably just really good at hiding it.

Nobody likes to think that they're easy to resist.

Chapter Twenty-Five

December 23, 6 p.m.

The board games take over the lounge with the adults playing too. There's a very serious game of Monopoly that isn't helped by the pot of warm mulled wine on the table, which has replaced the empty jug of bourbon hot chocolate.

I don't fancy having to refinance the only street I have left because Courtney is building so many hotels, so I bail and help Linda prepare the buffet supper in the kitchen, away from the rowdy revelers.

She hands me a platter of cold meats. "So, tomorrow, I might need you to help with the farm work. Our friends are looking after the animals while we go down to town and see our respective partners — a little early Christmas date, if you like." She says it like every mom has lovers, as if it's a totally normal thing to do.

"You have two boyfriends, right?" *Am I being rude? If it's so normal, we can talk about it, can't we?* She doesn't seem bothered by my line of questioning.

She nods. "One of them lives too far away to visit, but the other runs a restaurant in town. He's making me a special lunch." She rubs her hands together in glee.

"We met him the other day, a very nice man. You're a lucky lady." I hesitate. "If you don't mind me asking, I've never seen Bob's partner. What's she like?"

She pulls more trays of food out of the pantry, handing them to me. Another feast for the five thousand.

"Oh, I don't mind. She's lovely — nothing like me at all, all elegant and businesslike." I know what she means. If you had to describe Linda, the word homely would come to mind. She wears sneakers all day and more often than not the only make-up she puts on is smudges of flour across her nose. It still hurts to see her compare herself in such a way, though, as if she's less pretty.

"He comes home to you, though." I put the trays down and start pulling the plastic wrap off.

Her face lights up as if I am talking about her crush, not her husband of thirty or so years. "He sure does, and he finds us both beautiful in our own unique ways. That's the joy of it."

"Linda, are you happy?" She seems to have everything she wants. *Does that make you happy though or do we always desire more?*

"Of course, honey. Are *you* happy?"

I giggle. "I am." She leans in, inquisitively, and raises her eyebrows. God, this family is something else. "Not just because of G, but for *lots* of reasons. Okay, we kissed, but nothing more, and I'm not going to tell you anything until there's something to tell."

She reaches her arms around me and hugs me so hard that my feet lift off the floor. Then she puts me back where she found me and lets me breathe again. "Oh, Soph, I'm so excited for you both. Fingers crossed."

"Where is he, anyway?" Not that I need to know where he is or anything, because we're taking time to think about how we want to move on, and I am perfectly fine not being with him twenty-four-seven. And that's what I hope his mom sees in my face—and not the fact that I kind of miss his hand on my back and his lips on my lips. She gets it.

Linda dives back into the pantry and starts bringing out bottles of wine. "Guillaume took my phone upstairs to make a call. He ordered something for Christmas, and I don't think it's turned up yet."

"That reminds me. I need my parcel." I'd wrapped up a load of gifts for G's close family and sent it here by courier. It was much more practical than bringing an extra suitcase. I hadn't planned to be there when they opened their gifts, but I am actually quite excited about it now. I've picked something out for his brothers and sisters and his parents too, and I just know they're going to love them.

Corkscrew in hand, she gets to work opening the bottles—one, then a second, then a third. "They have to breathe before we eat," she says, pointing at them. "That's very important, so take note. I'll get all the gifts out tomorrow night when Santa's been. Don't want to ruin it for the grands."

G joins us after his mysterious phone call and we carry everything through to the lounge. Courtney and

Monica have teamed up and created a real estate empire and everybody's bankrupt. It's probably a good time to feed the hordes.

I'd forgotten how neat G is. He sits and puts all the cards and play money back in the box exactly as you would have found it when it had been all new. Sure as hell, if I go upstairs right now, he'll have organized our two suitcases worth of clothes in the wardrobe as if they'd always been there.

I can't say that in twenty years I'll still find that endearing, but right now, it tickles me to see how conscientious he is about everything...even our relationship — how he's been to therapy, got his head in the right place before he commits to me.

Even his brain is tidy.

I've filled mine with a ton of new information recently. It's stuffed with thoughts and ideas. Although, as each day passes, the worries and stress are flying out of it, leaving more room for the good stuff.

Linda and I serve the food, we eat, then everybody just kind of chills out in front of the fire. G gets his guitar, and we all sing Christmas songs, ever so softly, while the snow drifts down outside.

I've only felt like this once or twice in my life, when we'd lain out in the clearing in the middle of summer and the air brushed over our bodies, the bees had buzzed around us and all my worries had floated away with the breeze.

That feeling, the weightlessness of being content, is so relaxing. I no longer need to be alone with G to sense it. I am surrounded by people, all packed into a compact living room. Monica's legs are strewn across mine and one of the grands is slowly drifting off to sleep in my arms, cuddling the cat.

After a while, we all stretch and yawn and make our way to bed. Thibault picks up his sons, one in each arm, and carries them out to the car. G and I help Linda tidy up, despite her protestations that she can do it all on her own.

Then we climb the stairs up to the attic room, leaving the warmth of the first floor behind us. G's hand accompanies my back up the stairs. Fatigue has gotten the better of me. He's pretty much holding me up. We get changed, separately, and snuggle under the sheets and blankets, hunkering down for warmth.

I push down the pillow wall to see G's face. "I'm so cold," I say, through chattering teeth.

"We could huddle together for warmth."

"Don't think I don't know what you're up to. The pillow wall is there for a reason." *To stop me from caving.* And now, apparently, to stop him too. *Ugh. We're ridiculous.*

"You have a thick pair of fleece pajamas and one of my sweatshirts on. Nothing's going to get through that." He has a point, and I don't want to get hypothermia, not at Christmas. A little huddling is the sensible thing to do. We're grown adults. And it's a survival technique, not cuddling.

I pull the pillow wall out of the bed and throw my body against his. "Better?" he asks, his voice muffled by my sweatshirt hood.

"Oh my God, you are so warm." I nuzzle into him, and he wraps his arms tightly around me, pinning my head to his chest. I push my legs between his, sink my hands under his T-shirt and hold him to me. Despite the layers, I can feel him harden against me. "Really? *This* is doing it for you?" I say, chuckling.

He shifts around. "I can't help it. It's your hands on my body. You don't know what that does to me. It's got a mind of its own."

Flattering but useless, I am not doing anything that involves exposing flesh. "Well, tell it to calm its shit, because even if I did want to have sex with you, there's no way I'm going to take a single layer of clothing off. Nothing's penetrating these pants tonight."

He kisses the top of my head. "It won't listen to me. Tell it to its face."

"Funny."

He chuckles. "Ah, it was worth a try." The radiator gurgles and bubbles behind us. "Dad's going to turn the heating up tonight, so it should be much warmer by tomorrow. It takes a little time to really get going. One-hundred-year-old French plumbing, unfortunately."

And warmer it is. As the night progresses, we rolled to our sides. Around two a.m., the sweatshirts come off, and around three it's warm enough to stick a foot and an arm out of the covers. By four we're both out of the covers with pajamas unbuttoned.

Five a.m. finds us naked and curled up in each other's arms again.

A few minutes later involves some tentative kisses on the back of my neck and an, *"are you asleep?"* in my ear.

I suggest, perhaps, to him that a hand should sink between my legs…because I'm weak. And that hand gives good orgasms.

"It's officially Christmas Eve," he whispers in my ear. "Have you been a good girl?"

"If you make a joke about my chimney, you get thrown out of bed," I reply, gasping as he plunges his fingers inside me.

"What about my North Pole?" he replies, as I writhe into his touch.

"Stop it or Santa won't be coming this year." That earns me a loud laugh. "Shh, you'll wake everybody."

Silently, and with very little effort, he brings me to fruition. He knows my body, and he knows what I like. It's like coming home.

He kisses my neck again, takes away his hand and reaches behind me. "Do I need protection?"

"You haven't—?" I choke on the question. I want so bad to have sex right now, but if he's slept with anybody else, that changes everything. I haven't dared ask, and now is probably the worst time to find that out.

"No." His lips run across the nape of my neck. "You know you don't have to ask. There's only you."

"Then go, ho, ho." He enters me from behind, his whole body enveloping mine. Moaning in pleasure, he traces his hand down to my clit.

We make love, calmly and slowly, so as not to wake our neighbors. It's a quiet little quickie. Well, as quiet as you can be when you haven't made love for two months and you're having make up sex with the love of your life.

I put my hand over my mouth as he takes me there for the second time, riding him through it. He buries his mouth into my arched spine, grunting and gasping as he comes.

"Santa came," he says, rolling away.

I giggle. "Seriously?"

"Wait. I'm not finished. He filled your stocking."

I shake my head in despair and turn to snuggle into him. "What time is it? I feel like I haven't slept at all."

He pecks me on the lips. "Twenty past five. Go back to sleep, I'll help with the farm this morning, and you can take the afternoon shift." I'm quite sure I thanked him, although to be honest, I think I just fell fast asleep in his arms, comforted by hope and ignoring any niggling doubts.

"There's only you," he'd said. That's all I need to know.

Chapter Twenty-Six

Christmas Eve, midday.

The smell of bacon woke me and has me bundling up in several blankets before going down to the kitchen to investigate further.

"Good afternoon," says Monica. "You look rested. Did you sleep well?" I go to smile and realize that I already am. Somehow a permanent grin has etched itself onto my face during the night.

"She *does* look cheerful," adds Courtney, putting down what she's doing and coming over to investigate. "Sophie is never this happy before coffee."

"She *isn't*. She must have slept *really* well...or not at all." Their sarcasm is on point this morning. *Is it still morning?*

I pull out a stool and sit down, ignoring the two clucking hens before me. "Ooh, coffee," I say, trying to wipe the stupid smirk off my face. "Yes, please."

It doesn't work. The smile will not give. I'm busted.

G walks in, three-year-old Chloe sitting on his shoulders, a handful of straw in her hand. "Hey," he says, with a grin as wide as mine.

The twins point and gasp. "You guys f — " Courtney stops herself short. Their guests are standing right there. "No way!"

"I don't know what you're talking about," I reply, my face like a Cheshire cat.

G shakes his head. "What? I slept like a baby, visions of sugar plums dancing in my head."

"Sure," says Monica, rolling her eyes in despair at the two of us and getting back to her cooking. "Get washed up. We're eating in ten minutes."

G puts Chloe down, and she shows me the straw. "*Paille pour Jesus*," she says walking over to Bob and Linda's porcelain nativity and giving Jesus the comfiest of beds.

She explains each figurine to me, in great detail, in incomprehensible French, until G comes back, all clean. "*Va laver tes mains avec Maman, c'est bientôt à table*," he says to her, and she runs off to clean up too. He turns to me and wraps his hands around my waist, "Hey, you."

"Hey." Looks like we aren't making a secret of what happened last night, whatever that means.

He stifles a yawn. "Did you get some sleep? I'm exhausted."

I peck him on the lips. "Yes. Thank you. I'll swap with you this afternoon. You can have a long nap. Big night tonight."

"Is Santa coming again?" he asks, before kissing me back.

"Mmhmm-m. For real this time."

"Ugh, get a room." Monica pushes past us. "Food's up. Put each other down and come eat."

The afternoon is spent with the goats, me cleaning out their pen and them making it all dirty again and butting me in the behind in the process.

Personal note—tick 'goat farmer' off my list of potential jobs.

As soon as I've finished and showered, the twins rope me into preparing food for the evening. There's no sign of Bob and Linda, so their afternoons must be going very well.

"You can do the potatoes if you like. I seem to remember you're pretty good at it." Courtney hands me a pot and a peeler

I sit down at the counter. "Oh my God, I must have peeled like two hundred potatoes for that weekend, easily."

"So, you're back with Gil, then?"

Whoa, okay. Right in there with the important stuff. Courtney, bless her. Always straight to the point.

I stick my pot under the tap, filling it with water. "Honestly, I don't know. We've talked about what we both want, but I don't know if we really know where we're going. That doesn't really answer your question, does it?"

She laughs. "Nope." I grab my peeler and get to work.

"Put simply, I'm about to go off and travel for several months, then I'm going to settle down somewhere and work from home. Your brother has a burgeoning career in acting, which means he is going to be working for the foreseeable future—like, all the time."

She grabs her own peeler, sits in front of me and starts working on the carrots. "So, what are you going to do?" *What am I going to do? Who the fuck knows?* Not me. G's probably clueless too.

"I don't know. We can't stay away from each other, but we can't be together. We'll never see each other."

"So that's it. You're going to just break his heart? Again."

Oof, okay. That hurts.

I put down my potato and place my hands on the counter, looking her straight in the eye. "No. I don't know. Maybe he's breaking mine." I sigh. Can't we just enjoy the *now*? Isn't that what G always says when he quotes his favorite author? I haven't read the books and I don't know the theory behind it, but if we can move on from the past, maybe we don't have to think about the future, either. "Today G and I are in love and we're happy. So, let's just deal with today."

We're interrupted by Bob and Linda busting into the kitchen, their arms filled with crates full of food.

"Hey, guys." Linda puts down her crate and surveys the three of us hard at work. "All my girls in the kitchen, working hard, makes me so happy."

"Don't get used to it, Mom," says Courtney. "We're just helping out."

Bob sticks his arm around his wife's shoulder. "Well, I think it's sweet, you all cooking for a change, giving your mom a rest. I'd like to see it more often."

The twins are twenty-four-year-old women, but they roll their eyes and stomp their feet like teenagers at the idea of having to do any extra chores.

It occurs to me that I'm so happy to help because I've never done it. They've been pitching-in their entire lives. I can see where having a close-knit family would be a chore in its own right. I still want everything that they have, though—responsibilities and all. Family is priceless.

G wanders into the kitchen in just his jeans, half asleep. He scratches his abs, pecks me on the lips and heads to the fridge, where he pulls out the milk carton and drinks straight from it.

"Guillaume!"

The twins cross their arms and sulk some more.

All we're missing is Thibault rolling in after curfew, smelling of cigarettes, and the perfect family picture would be complete. I should take a photo for their Christmas card.

We help unpack the food. Okay, G and I do it. The twins take the opportunity to slink away and get ready for tonight's festivities.

Evening is drawing in and Thibault, his wife and the grands will be here soon. Bob's cousin and his wife have come back after their afternoon stroll, trying to tire out little Chloe. The twins' boyfriends and their parents are due in an hour. It's everyone to help, as usual, to lay the table for Christmas Eve dinner, wrap any last-minute gifts and get the food in the oven.

G gets dressed and goes off to do secret gift stuff with his dad. I'm not allowed to take part.

"Do you mind if I nip away and get changed?" I ask Linda. Oversized jumper, jeans, and fluffy socks aren't going to cut it for the most wonderful time of the year.

She smiles. "Of course not. Thanks for your help today."

I put a hand on her shoulder. "Thank you for letting me be a part of your family."

"As I said before, anyone who wants in in this crazy family is always welcome."

I wrap my arms around her. "You've been more of a mother to me in the short time I've known you than my mother ever was."

"She doesn't know what she's missing," she replies.

"Ooh, hugs!" Bob and G run into the kitchen and dive in on our hug until we're all octopus arms again. I love it. I never want to let any of these people go.

G accompanies me up the stairs again, this time with his hand on my butt. "I can get changed on my own."

"I know. I'm not going to bother you. I'm just going to watch."

Oh yeah? "Pervert."

He chuckles and gives my butt a little squeeze. "You love it."

I walk into the room and pull off my jumper while G just sits back on the bed and watches. "You're really just going to watch me get changed?"

"You're wearing the necklace I gave you."

"Of course I am. It's going to go everywhere with me from now on. I'll always have a piece of you, wherever I wake up." His face drops. "Nope, don't get somber on me, it's frickin' Christmas, G. Food and fun and gifts and magic." I crawl on to the bed and up to his sad little face. "Kiss me."

"You see, you do love it when I watch."

I peck him on the lips. "Don't push your luck."

* * * *

All prettied up, and maybe a little sexed up too, we join everybody else. I try not to let the sex glow show, but the twins roll their eyes again, and I give up pretending.

There's old-timey Christmas music playing, and the grands are dancing out the last of their energy. The chimney has stockings hung up on it, with all the families' names, including the grands and Chloe. Thibault's stocking has had his wife's name embroidered on it a while back and G's has a little post-it note with 'and Sophie too' written on it. *Bless them.*

A couple of gifts have made it under the tree, but the majority will appear overnight as we sleep, as is the tradition in this house. I've gone to great lengths to pay someone to wrap and label all my gifts, with fancy ribbons and fake holly, thinking I wouldn't be here to see them open them, and now it just seems trite. I want to unwrap them and wrap them again myself, so they won't look too fancy among Linda's hand-wrapped ones.

The delicious scent of boeuf bourguignon, potatoes and carrots bubbling away in the kitchen is wafting into my nose and making me hungry. It isn't like there isn't already a ton of finger food on the coffee table and, as with every party in the Carter household, a crate of Champagne. We aren't going to starve tonight.

In the dining room, their finest crystal and best plates have all been gotten out of storage and cleaned. There are fancy serviettes and holly and ivy brought in from outside. It's magical. The table has been extended. Once again, we're going to be so many at the table, chattering and laughing.

My stomach turns as I think about the fact that I'll be leaving this place in a couple of days. I grasp onto the corner of the table and take a deep breath. *They'll always be here for me, right?* When G and I come to the inevitable conclusion that we'll have to go back to our lives, I don't want to lose my precious found family. Even though, when it comes down to it, they were never really mine, only by association. When G finds love again, I'll most likely not be welcome, no matter how much they appreciate me.

I shake away the tears forming in my eyes. Today is today. We'll let tomorrow do its thing, and I'll see how it goes from there.

Chapter Twenty-Seven

Christmas Day, 5 a.m.

We are woken at five by the grands jumping on our bed and announcing that Santa has been. Luckily, we'd worn pajamas, G having explained that this, too, would be part of the Carter Christmas ritual. Last night the food and company had been sublime, and we'd all gone off to bed quite early, except for the twins and their boyfriends, who'd sat around the fire-pit, in the snow, looking at the stars and trying to spot Santa.

My boyfriend had fallen asleep gripping me so tightly that I could hardly breathe. Did he feel the sense of impending doom that I did? We hadn't talked about it. The elephant in the room was keeping his trunk firmly knotted until Christmas was over.

I feel it, through to my bones — like the moment he'd gotten up to leave on Halloween or that stolen kiss on opening night — as if someone is grabbing on to my heart to stop it from beating.

G is my heartbeat. Without him, I can't breathe.

We lumber down the stairs as the boys bound down in front of us and go off to join the rest of the groggy adults who are glugging down coffee and trying to look cheerful about being woken up at such an hour.

"Merry Christmas, ya fi—" says G, winking at me.

"Don't you finish that sentence, young man," said Linda, giving him the stern mom look that she has mastered so well. She's a formidable mother when she wants to be.

He looked down at his feet, suitably chastised and whispers, "…filthy animals."

The boys run back in and pull us all into the living room. There are heaps of gifts everywhere. The kids have the biggest piles, but there's at least one for each of the grown-ups too.

Christmas had been a much more somber affair when I was a kid. I wasn't deprived, in any way. I always got what I asked for, but there wasn't the magic that I could feel in this room now.

Love. This is what family feels like. A touch snarky, irritated with each other, a little grumpy from too little sleep and too many people in one house—but ultimately, love.

The grip on my heart tightens. *Fuck.*

We sit and wait and watch as the kids rip open gift after gift until they have completely filled the room with paper and toys. Then the adults started opening theirs.

"Sophie!" The twins scream my name out in unison as they opened their gifts. I've gone for scarves and bags for them and their sister-in-law. It's a bit boring, but you always need a nice going-out bag. I might not have thought through the fact that these guys don't exactly wear Gucci, though. Thibault's wife's eyes widen, and she hugs it to her chest, like she normally does with her babies. I smile at them all. *Awkward.* I hadn't meant to outshine. It has been a while since I'd bought gifts.

My cheeks redden, and I rest my head on G's chest, away from their happy faces.

"I went overboard, didn't I?" I whisper to G. There's nothing I hate more than people who flaunt their wealth. When you've got a ton of money in the bank, it's so easy to waste it. I'd not grown up like that.

Grandma had made my costumes for the pageants, and my parents had lived simply. I'd paid off their home when I was sixteen, as a thank you for all they'd done for me. I didn't tell them, not wanting to cause a fuss, so we'd never acknowledged it, but I'm sure they were happy about it.

He peers down into my hidden face. "No, it's fine. I think you made their Christmas." He wraps an arm tightly around me, reassuringly. "Are you going to open one of yours?"

The twins have bought me beautiful leather luggage labels and a traveling iron. Perfect. So thoughtful. Tears fill my eyes, and I swipe at them, shyly. *Someone must be cutting onions in here.*

Linda and Bob have given me a pile of books. "A cookery book?" I say, laughing. "You know this is just going to gather dust." I shake my head and laugh at her terribly misplaced faith in me.

"You'll see," replies Linda. "One day you're going to want to know how long to roast a chicken for or how to make bread — and you'll thank me."

I don't want to offend her. It is an awesome gift. *Stupid big mouth.* "I was kidding. I love it, and I promise that once I'm settled down, I'll invite you over for dinner."

"Bring your own Pepto," says G, earning him a look of disdain from his mother, who is busily unwrapping my gift.

"Sophie!" Now it's Linda's turn to cry out my name. "Oh, you shouldn't have." I'd gotten her one of those auto cookers, the best one on the market.

I shrug, smiling. It's the obvious gift. If ever someone was deserving of one of these, it's the woman who is chained to the oven three hundred and sixty-five days a year. "I figured you could take some time for yourself occasionally and let this thing do the work." She's grinning from ear to ear. I've made the right choice.

I hand G his gift. "Didn't think I'd be giving you this in person." I rub my hands together. *Have I done good? Will he love it? Of course, he's going to love it.*

It is literally the perfect gift. I could not have done better.

"It feels like an envelope. Did you make me a card?" he asks, jokingly shaking it next to his ear.

The whole family turns to look and see what I've given him. I'm getting a reputation for giving good gifts, and this, theoretically, has to be the best one.

He takes his time opening it, infuriating his sisters, who are losing patience. They looked very disappointed when they saw that it was just an envelope. He rips it open and pulls out the contents.

My breath hitches. *Like it. Oh God, please like it.*

"What does it say, Gil," asks Courtney, who can't cope anymore. "What *is* it?"

G looks at me with those big soft brown eyes, tears forming in both of them, and I breathe the hugest sigh of relief. Then the biggest, boldest kiss lands on my lips. "I can't believe it. I can't believe you did this for me. Thank you." He turns to his family, shaking his head, trying to comprehend what is happening right now. "It's tickets to a retreat with Eckhart Tolle."

Jaws drop. "No way. Oh my God, Sophie. He's been driving us mad with this stuff for I don't know how long. You nailed it."

"She did," he replies, his head still wagging in disbelief. "I get to meet him, right?"

I nod. "Yes, of course. You've got a little time to work on your poker face, so he doesn't think you're a stalker or something." My heart is bursting with joy.

Linda passes me her gift. "This is a little something extra from me and Bob." It's a small bag with a box inside containing a beautiful silver bracelet, engraved with the letter S. "All my kids have one with their initial—and the grands. It's a family thing. Whatever happens"—she looks at her son and gives an embarrassed smile—"whatever happens, you will always be welcome here. You'll always have your French Mom and Dad to come home to if it all gets to be overwhelming. Okay?"

I don't reply. It's all way too much for me to handle, my eyes stinging from the held back tears. I don't want to cry on Christmas, so I smile and thank her, and let G puts it on my wrist. Then, when everything has calmed down, I give her and Bob the biggest, soppiest, soggiest hugs.

Present giving over, we start the business of clearing everything up and getting the table laid for breakfast. There's bacon and eggs and pancakes. Honestly, I'm not sure I have room for any more food in my already-full stomach, but as usual, it smells so good that I'm left no choice but to dig in.

Chapter Twenty-Eight

Christmas Day, midday

Once breakfast is over, everybody converges around me. Linda hands me a little parcel.

The tag reads, 'It's for next year. For your private thoughts and so you can write shit about people, and they won't know.'

I giggle and blush. He knows what I write about in my journal.

"Open it," she adds. "It's from Guillaume." *I'd kind of guessed.*

There's an inscription on the front page. 'Shee, for all the things we're going to do together, love, G,' and there's a Post-it note telling me to get my boots on and go outside.

I'm half expecting him to have saddled up Tornado so we can go for a llama ride. What can possibly be outside in three feet of snow on Christmas Day?

I step outside and look around for him.

Then I see it.

Parked in the car park is a beautifully restored lime green VW camper. G is standing in front of it — or rather hopping around trying to keep warm — holding out the keys.

"What?" *What the fuck?* This can't be it. "This is for *me*?"

"No," said G as he walks toward me with the keys, "this is for us."

"What?" *What?* My hands started trembling. *What is going on?*

He places his hand on my back, warm and comforting, despite the cold, and leads me toward the van, opens the front door and sits me in the passenger seat. Then he ambles around and gets in the driver's seat.

I put my quivering hand to my mouth, trying to stop myself from once again falling into a pile of soppy tears, and he places his hands on mine, gripping tightly and pulling them down into his lap. "I know you have a million questions, and once you're over the shock, you're going to give me another million reasons as to why we shouldn't do this — because of my career and how you'll never forgive yourself or I'll never forgive you if I give it up — but hear me out."

I nod. "I'm listening." I can't do much else. I've lost the capacity for speech.

He gulps and takes a deep breath, stares deep into my eyes and smiles, as if he has found what he's looking for. "From the first moment I met you, I knew that you weren't just another person who was going to come and go in my life. I knew you'd have an impact on me somehow. You're the chaos to my calm — except, inside, I've always been chaotic. You made it bubble to the surface until I had to go sort it all out. For that, I'll always be grateful. You made me realize I can love somebody and not feel like it's the worst thing in the world."

My heart is beating so fast that my ears are ringing. *What is this? Is he coming with me? What is going on?* "Okay."

"Then you decided to take your life into your own hands, make decisions for yourself for the first time ever, despite being on your own for so long. I'm so proud of you for that. Your GED, your studies? That's so amazing. Then, this trip, traveling and taking time to find out what you want from life. I'm in awe of you, Sophie Smith. You make me so happy every day, and I'm so proud that you chose me, when you could have had anybody."

I try to get any words out and all I can say is, "I love you."

He looks into the van, almost as if he's seeing it for the very first time. "I bought this two weeks ago. Can you imagine? Then, because of the snow, they couldn't get it here, and I thought that you wouldn't get it. I was going to ask my parents to give it to you and let you decide if you wanted me to come along. I wrote a letter and everything. But you're here, and I'm here, and we're in love, and I can do this in person. So, take me with you, Shee. Take me around Europe and let me love you. Let me share this with you."

"But your job?" *Ugh. No, no, no, this is my dream, not his.* I want to scream at him for wanting to give everything up for me.

"My job can wait. A few months ago, you said, "*I would have followed you around the world,*" and it made me think. You know, why should you have to do that?

Why can't I? Now look… I'm throwing this at you on Christmas Day, in front of everybody, and it's big. You can say 'no' and I won't hold it against you at all. If this is something you want to do alone, take the camper and do it." He pauses.

I did say that, about following him anywhere. If I was willing to do that, then I should be willing to let him do it for me. He's giving me the love I so crave, a family, a new start, and he wants to come along for the ride. I'd be a fool to walk away from this man a second time.

"Yes. Of course, yes. Yes. Come with me. Hold my hand. Teach me French. Make love to me under the stars at the foot of the Appalachian Mountains."

He cringes. "They're in America…"

"The Alps?"

"Sierra Nevada?" he suggests, grinning at my confused face. "It's in Spain."

I jump around in my seat. "Ooh, Spain. Can we go to Spain?"

"Wherever you want to go. In fact, I'd make love to you right here, but it's way too cold." He laughs and rubs my shoulders, bringing me in for a hug.

"It's perfect, G, so perfect." I look over his shoulder and his family are all jumping up and down, trying to keep warm. "I think they're waiting for us to say something."

He opens the door. "She said yes!"

They all cheer and immediately run back inside to get warm. I take a moment to inspect the van. It looks brand new. There's a little table and a couch, which I assume turns into a bed and there are cupboards and a sink. "I love it."

He points things out. "I made a bookshelf, for your books, and I'm going to have to find out a way to get all your clothes in, but we should be good."

I don't care about my clothes. I'll leave them all here if I have to, just grab a pair of jeans and a T-shirt and forget the rest.

This is wild. I'm in love and I'm free. Next year is going to be amazing. I hold on to G and listen to him telling me all the things this little van does until our feet start to go numb. Then we decide that we're going to move the camper into a barn for the night, do more exploring and preparing tomorrow.

* * * *

Christmas Day, just before midnight

So, it turns out G was wrong. I didn't write that much shit about people in this journal. I wrote down my thoughts, like, a lot, and I may have talked about sex more than anybody reading this wanted me too. Or maybe they did?

I found love, I found a family and I found meaning in my life. I lost a lot of things on the way, too — my resentment, my career, my fear of intimacy. Okay, I'm still working on that last one. But the most important thing that happened to me was that I became loved. I hadn't known I was missing it, didn't know I needed it, but now that I have it, I'm not going to let it go.

Epilogue

August 22, 7 a.m.

The knock on the door wakes me from the most amazing dream. I sit up in bed and look around the van. Where are we? I step down into the van and climb over the piles of clean washing that need to be put away.

Oh yeah, that's where we are.

"Fresh coffee and croissants," I say as I bring in the tray and climb back into bed. The croissants are still warm and flaky and giving off the most delicious aroma. You don't get this kind of quality breakfast in every part of the world. This was made especially for us.

"Mm-m." A hand runs down my back and settles on the base of my spine. "Did you say fresh coffee?"

"Uh-huh." He sighs the sigh of a man who hasn't had a decent coffee in a long while. I pass him my cup. He takes a sip and hands it back. "And homemade croissants." He reaches over my shoulder and grabs one. "G, you'll get crumbs in the bed."

"Sorry." He sticks his palm under the croissant but continues to eat.

Breakfast in bed has become a bit of a daily occurrence in the van. I regularly shake out the sheets after my messy other half has gotten crumbs everywhere. The thing is, the table kind of holds up the bed, so you can only have one or the other. Van life is cramped, but when you're parked next to a beautiful sandy beach or with a view of the mountains as far as the eye can see, you don't give two fucks about a few crumbs on your pillow.

"Eat up. We've got a ton of things to do today. The wedding's tomorrow and your mom gave us a list of chores longer than my arm."

He mumbles something incoherent, then swallows his food and speaks again. "I think I have to get fitted for my suit. You'll have to take my place."

There's no way in hell I'm doing the chicken coop...or the goats.

"Dress and suit fittings are just before lunch. That'll give you plenty of time to go clean out the chickens." I sip my coffee and run my hand down the thigh that is emerging from the sheets. "Where did your pajamas go?"

"Too hot for pajamas. What are you going to do while I'm doing all that?"

"I'm going to catch up with my first love. He's tall, dark and handsome, and he left me for a camel."

G kisses my back and leans over for another croissant. "He was a fool." I tap his hand. "Hey, I'm going to need energy for everything we've got to get done today — and what I'm about to do right now." He removes the coffee mug from my hand, places it on the tray and pulls me back down into bed, kissing me with croissant-covered lips.

We've been fooling around for ten minutes when the door knocks.

"What?" I shout. We were just getting to the good bit. Everybody knows that when the van's a rockin'...

"It's me, Courtney. We've got a problem." I stand up again, this time grabbing something a little more decent to cover myself up with.

"What's up?" I ask, opening the door.

A very stressed, very pregnant, Courtney stands in front of me. We aren't the only ones who'd gotten frisky at Christmas. "The wedding's off."

"What?" We've driven for three days to get here for their wedding.

"Monica has just gone into labor and my water has just broken from the stress." She is holding her very large belly, as if the baby is going to drop out any minute.

"What?" says G from behind me.

I looked down at her belly. "Neither of you are due for another couple of weeks. You're both getting married tomorrow."

"Oww." She laughs through the pain. "I don't think the babies get that. I think you — *aaahhh* — need to take me to the hospital."

"What?" says G *again*, jumping out of bed, stubbing his toe and sending the camper into a rocking frenzy as he leaps around with his foot in his hand. "Right now?"

We sit Courtney down outside in one of our folding chairs and quickly throw some clothes on.

Life with the Carters never runs smoothly, but that's half the fun of it.

It looks like my little reunion with Tornado will have to wait. It's time for some more grands.

Want to see more from this author?
Here's a taster for you to enjoy!

Mixed Emotions: (Not)Normal
Katy Hunter

Coming April 2022

Excerpt

"So I told him…goodbyyyyye!"

I keep the last note going as long as I can, but it wavers a little toward the end. A warm-up might have been a good idea, since my voice is seriously out of practice. Yesterday's rehearsal was the first time I've sung on stage since God knows when. The crowd erupts, and I thank my lucky stars that this has been a success. This gig is brimming with A-list performers and I'm a has-been—C-list at the very most.

"Milly! Milly! Milly!" roars the crowd, wanting more.

"Thank you! Thank you so much!" I point at the crowd. I'm nothing without them.

There's no reason for any of the people out there to be cheering so loudly. But they love it. Maybe it's nostalgia, or I've just lucked out and a few of my old fans are in the crowd. Whatever it is, it's exhilarating. I'm on a high that it's going to be difficult to come down from.

For a second I want to go back. My brain wipes away the bad memories, and I forget about how much I hate touring and management and the invasion of my privacy. I want to stay up on this stage forever, absorb all this positive emotion, sing the songs that I love.

The lights come up and I thank the audience then my honorary musicians. They offered to come along and play today out of the kindness of their hearts. Anything for a good cause. They are a mix of guys I've worked with in the past and a couple of friends of friends. They're good people.

What if I hired them, wrote some songs, went on a short tour? *Nothing* beats this feeling.

The call to do such an impressive charity show was a surprise. I'd given up everything to go off to college for a couple of years, finish my education, but I take the occasional gig here and there. I never made as much money as everybody thinks I did—just enough to get by and some savings put aside for traveling. I'm not poor, but my bank account can always do with topping up.

"Thank you, Milly," says Zane, the compere for the evening. He walks out onto the stage and over to me, grabbing my arm to keep me here. "A little birdy tells me that you recently finished college and that you're about to do some traveling."

Uh-huh. I nod, nervously. *Where's he going with this?* I don't exactly talk about my private life, especially now. I'm not *'Milly the celebrity'* anymore. I gave that up.

"Yeah," I reply. "And?"

"Well, this little birdy told me that he wants to come, too." *Zane wants to travel with me?*

Oh, no. No, no, make it stop. He's pointing off to the side of the stage where my boyfriend, or rather future *ex*-boyfriend, is striding into the spotlight.

My stomach sinks and I kind of want it to pull me down and under the stage. I glance down at my feet. *Trap doors. Do they still have them? Nope, apparently not.* Zane's hand is still firmly gripping my arm, stopping me from going anywhere. This is great publicity for their show. These days it's not enough to have amazing singers. You've got to have a little gossip and scandal, too. I'm about to give them the latter.

"No." I grit my teeth and turn to Zane, still smiling. If the million phone cameras pointed at me right now are any good, they have to be capturing the sheer horror in my eyes. That'll be online before you can blink.

My boyfriend, beautiful as he is, is about to discover rejection in front of all these people, and he has only himself to blame. I wrench my arm from Zane's grip and stroll over toward him. The grin on my about-to-be-ex's face is priceless. He must think he's *so* clever, doing this here. However this ends—as he well knows—this is going to give him that much-sought-for step up into the limelight.

"Don't do it," I say through my gritted smile.

He lifts a microphone to his mouth, drops to one knee and holds out a ring.

Fuck.

I block out everything—the sound of the crowd, the roadies crouching down beside and around me trying to empty the stage without getting in the way. I block out Zane as he does some kind of running commentary. I ignore the man at my feet.

Funnily enough, the hardest thing to shut out is the voice in the back of my mind that keeps repeating, *If you say no, Mum's going to kill you.* She's watching this right now. My whole family is. In fact, if I wasn't trying to block it out, too, I'd know this from the fact that I can hear her ringtone coming from my back pocket as I try so hard to make myself disappear.

He begins to speak and the crowd hushes. "Milly. I've known you for less than a year, but when you find the love of your life, you just know." *If you knew anything after 'less than a year' then you'd know that this is a terrible, awful idea.* "I love you and I want to spend the rest of my life with you."

I close my eyes and breathe in and out. Trying to make myself disappear didn't work. I'm still here. The earth didn't swallow me up. I did not float away. I am going to have to deal with this in the only way I can. It's not going to be pretty.

I step forward, clasp the ring, the box, his hand and push it toward him. "No," I say, only loud enough for him to hear. "I told you that I didn't want a wedding or babies or forever. You knew this."

"You… You don't love me?"

I shake my head. "No."

"You don't want to marry me? But…I love you."

"No." Anger swells inside me and it takes all I've got not to shove him off this stupid stage. *How dare you do this to me?* "Fuck off, just *fuck off!*"

He face forms this sort of vengeful, hurt scowl. "You were just using me for my body."

Yes. Have you seen your body? Of course I was. Well, that's not entirely true. I enjoyed his company, somewhat, and we had fun. Not 'get married and have babies' fun, but it wasn't *that* casual.

"Yes?" I reply, not wanting to go into the details.

A collective gasp comes from the crowd. The microphone is picking up everything I'm saying. *Oh,*

God. I scan the audience, trying to find at least one person nodding and giving me a thumbs-up.

Somebody out there gets this, right? They get that I don't want this, that there's nothing wrong with me for saying no, for being so shocked at the damned cheek of such an intimate, unwarranted, undesired moment being shared with the whole damn world.

Especially when he *knew* I'd say no. How can he think that I'd say yes? I made myself very, *very* clear.

Argh. I'm faced with a crowd of romantics, their hearts breaking into collective pieces in empathy with the man in front of me. He drops his head, followed by his hand, the ring box tumbling to the ground. His second knee sinks to the ground, and he folds up into a big, bawling pile of sad.

Shit. I can't do this. I turn, but Zane is heading for me, so I turn back and leap over my now-ex, who is prostrate on the floor. The crowd does a collective *'what-the-fuck?'* sound.

Did I really just jump over the man I turned down? Yes. Yes, I did.

I take one last look back at the mess I've left on stage and I run away, past the people offstage, their expressions as gobsmacked as the audience. I run to my trailer, grab my stuff, ignoring my manager who tries to block my exit, screaming things at me about *'responsibility'* and *'pleasing the public'*. I run out of there, out of the VIP area, past the crowds, the marketing stands and straight to the car park.

Out of breath and out of my mind, I rip open my car door and throw myself and my stuff into the car. I lock the doors and drive myself out of that place as quickly as the exiting traffic will allow. Only when I'm gone, when I can pull over, do I stop and breathe and cry huge, racking sobs as I'm slumped over the steering wheel.

I should never have come back. This is not my life anymore. I have things to do with my life that don't include any of these people. I need to get away. I need to be alone.

I get it. I'm not normal. I'm not like them.

About the Author

Katy Hunter lives on a mountain in France with her husband, kids and two dogs.

When she's not writing you can find her curled up in front of the fire, book in one hand and a glass of chardonnay in the other.

Katy loves to hear from readers. You can find her contact information, website details and author profile page at https://www.totallybound.com

Home of Erotic Romance

Sign up for our newsletter and find out about all our romance book releases, eBook sales and promotions, sneak peeks and FREE romance books!